ONE YEAR STAND WITH A PHILLY BILLIONAIRE 3

YONA

One Year Stand With A Philly Billionaire 3

Copyright © 2023 by Yona

All rights reserved.

Published in the United States of America.

Published by Cole Hart Signature, LLC.

Mailing List

To stay up to date on new releases, plus get information on contests, sneak peeks, and more,

Go To The Website Below...

www.colehartsignature.com

CHAPTER ONE

NAKARI

WHERE WE LEFT OFF...

I pulled up to DeJuan's favorite motel and parked my car on the side street. Days Inn was our meeting place. The high I had experienced with him was something I needed to do one more time before I made my next move.

I fixed myself up in the car mirror before stepping out and strutting all the way to the room number he had texted me. I knocked on the door about three to four times. Just when I turned to leave, he opened it.

"Hey, you gon' take that off?" I asked as soon as I walked into the room.

DeJuan handed me the blunt, which I knew was laced with that good stuff, and I took a pull. Instantly, I got that high that felt too good to be true.

"No. I wanted you to do it for me," he challenged as I took another pull.

I let the door close behind me as I slowly walked over to

him while chewing on my bottom lip. Yes, the shit was kicking in because DeJuan was no longer a sight to see.

I placed my hands under his shirt and pulled it over his head. Then I let my hand trace across his stomach and travel across his dick. Grabbing the smoke from him, I took another pull. I needed to be higher than a giraffe's ass to do this. Once my body started to feel extremely loose, I knew I was high.

Going back to my mission, I unzipped his pants and pushed them down with his boxers. I then turned around and pulled off my leather coat, letting it fall to the floor. I had no clothes on under it. DeJuan grabbed me and kissed my neck, sending a wave of electricity through my body, just like he had done before. I grabbed the belt from my coat and wrapped it loosely around his neck. He eased himself inside me and began to pump fast.

"You make my dick feel so good." He breathed.

I had to admit his dick was nice, and it felt even better.

"You want another hit?" he questioned.

Instead of answering him, I wrapped my legs around his waist and started to match his strokes. Grabbing the smoke, I lit it and took another pull before placing it to his lips, and he did the same. I let it fall, but I wasn't sure where it went.

I raised my hips, grinding back into him as I held onto the rope, yanking it a few times. DeJuan started humping me too good for my liking.

"It fell," I tried to tell him, but DeJuan pulled out of me and then pushed back inside, erasing the words that were about to leave my mouth.

"What was you saying?" he questioned and kissed me.

"Nothing. God, I was not saying nothing," I managed to get out between moans.

Hell, I really didn't remember what I was about to say.

DeJuan lifted my legs and held onto them as he pushed

into me. I placed my hand on the wall and met him in the middle, stroke after stroke. This was the best dick I ever had in my life, and if it was the drugs, I wouldn't mind taking them before sex every time.

"Harder! Harder!" I urged him.

DeJuan wrapped my legs around his neck, giving himself more access to my insides. My nails punctured the sheets as he dug into my insides.

"Oouuu. Oouu, slow down!" I cried.

DeJuan was fucking the shit out of me—something I was not used to. When he pushed my legs further back, I placed my hands on his waist to hold him back some.

"Move your hands." He swatted my hands away and continued to pound.

"DeJuan, something is burning!" I screamed and held onto him as I came hard.

I could smell the smoke and was starting to see it. I was high, but not that damn high. DeJuan was in a world of his own because he kept laying the pipe. He did a dip that had me clutching the sheets and closing my eyes. Then, he slid out of me and flipped me over. My ass was in the air, and he licked back and forth between my ass and my coochie, making me cum all over the place.

Finally, he picked me up, wrapping my legs around his waist as he moved us toward the bathroom. He held my hands straight against the door until I let go of his hands and wrapped my arms around his neck. I used my leg strength to help me ride him while we stood. This shit felt so good.

I grabbed the belt around his neck and pulled it some while I moved my hips in a slow, rocking motion. DeJuan began to bounce me on him, causing my head to fall on his shoulder. I licked and sucked on his neck as his grip on my ass cheeks tightened. He placed us on the bed, keeping one arm under me to hold me up. The burning smell was growing, and I only smelled it when we were near the bed. Assuming it as the smell from the drugs we were doing, I focused back on the sex I needed.

"Wrap your legs back," he demanded, and I followed his directions.

DeJuan's thrusts were now long and deep. He bit his bottom lip as he took his free hand and began to rub my pearl.

"I'm about to fucking cum," I notified him.

DeJuan only humped me faster.

Grabbing the belt, I held it as tight as I could while he fucked me hard. He had his hand in my hand, and it felt like he was trying to get me off him. Just like the last time, my body locked up, and I started to cum. DeJuan stopped moving completely, which threw me off. I was exhausted, so I didn't complain about not finishing my nut.

I looked over at the window and saw a cloud of smoke along with what looked like fire. Leaning over the side of the bed, I realized the sheet was on fire. As I looked around the room, I noticed the smoke detector was unplugged.

"Get up. It's a fire." I tapped DeJuan, but he did not move.

Panic set in my body when I called his name a few times, and he didn't say anything. I placed my finger under his nose, but I did not feel any air coming from him. Pushing his body off mine, I quickly gathered my things and ran out of the hotel room to my car.

Once inside, I sat there and watched the door. A couple of minutes went by before someone walking by stopped in front of the room. At that point, smoke had started to come from under the door, and I knew if everything didn't burn up, I would be fucked.

Moments later, a fire truck pulled up. While some got out and ran to the door, the others hooked up the fire hose. I watched as they broke the window, and a burst of flames came out. Another firefighter kicked the door down. They ran in and pulled out DeJuan's naked body. I watched them perform CPR until the paramedics pulled up. I knew once they all stood and someone came over with a white sheet, that I would need to figure things out.

My phone rang, and I picked it up. Amarie was FaceTiming me. Instead of answering, I sent her to voicemail. I knew that if my cousin ever found out the truth, she would be so hurt, which was why I drove myself to the hospital, slid into the clothes I had in my car, and checked in.

"Hey, someone slipped me something. I was at a bar, and I was smoking with some guy. Out of nowhere, I started feeling like I was in another world."

My plan was to meet DeJuan and have him confess to drugging me after getting him high out of his mind. It was never meant to end up like this.

"That's the girl right there from the motel, Officer," I heard a man say as he pointed to me.

It was the same man I saw at the motel.

CHAPTER TWO
AMARIE

I did my best not to show how upset I was about Nakari ignoring me. However, it had been about three days since I talked to her, and that was far too long. I was giving her space, but she wanted to disappear from everyone like she was invisible. I tried to ask Natalia about her, but she would just steer the conversation in another direction since she felt that Nakari was doing too much. Natalia had always gotten like that when Nakari and I would get in our feelings and want to shut the world out. Her favorite thing to say was we would eventually get over it.

Climbing out of my car, I used my key to let myself into Nakari's house. It was empty, and everything was turned off. She had decorated with her new furniture like she said, but she was not home, so I left back out and locked the door. I sat in my car and dialed her number, only to get the voicemail once again. Feeling like something was not right, I called my auntie.

"Yeah, baby." She answered the phone, sounding like she was out of breath.

"Have you talked to Nakari?" I asked.

"Yesterday. She said she was going somewhere. I'm gon' call you back," she said and hung up.

Knowing my auntie, she was somewhere getting her back blown out with her old nasty ass.

Frustrated, I drove back home. Nakari would reach out to me when she was ready, and I was not going to force it anymore. I had not done anything for her to feel like she needed to duck me. Pulling up to the entrance of my gated community, I entered the code and drove down the path to my house. I loved the new place and could live there forever. I couldn't wait to raise my kids there and make sure they never wanted anything.

My thoughts traveled to how I would now have to get all the work done that I possibly could before I pushed my baby out because I refused to miss a step in their life. I would be there for him or her through thick and thin. That was the promise I had already made to my child, and I was going to keep it.

Pulling up into my driveway, I shut my car off before using my key to enter the house. I had taken chicken out for dinner and decided to put it in the oven. I went into the kitchen, where I cleaned and seasoned my chicken before placing it in a pan and covering it with chicken broth. After I was done, I placed a lid on it and slid it into the oven. I would make some white rice and string beans to go with it.

While my chicken cooked, I started my bath. Filling the tub with hot water and a few drops of bubble bath, I wanted to soak my body and relax. I heard my phone ring while I was in the tub, but I decided to deal with it later. Everyone knew if it was an emergency to call twice. When the phone did not ring again, I knew that nothing was wrong.

Once I finished my bath, I turned the shower on and washed my body along with my hair, which had not been washed in weeks. The shower did not last long since my phone rang again. As I dried myself off, I figured Nakari had come to her senses and wanted to talk. Picking up my phone, I saw an unknown number and tossed it back down. Whoever that was could not have wanted me because I didn't talk to people who didn't have my number.

As I lay on my bed, I turned the TV on and watched a few minutes of the news. My city was crazy. Someone was always being killed, and lately, it had been more kids than adults. Once I had enough of that, I changed the channel just as they started talking about a fire in a rundown motel. That shit was nothing new to anyone around there. These bad ass kids were always setting shit off.

If I had a son, I would make sure he wasn't in the streets, and I would do my best to make him feel loved. Every day, I would make sure to let him know that no matter what he did in life, I would support him. Most people showered their daughters with love when their sons needed it more. Men, especially black men, had it harder than anyone on the streets. That's why, if I had a young black king, he would have street smarts as well as the knowledge that he didn't have to be out there. He would only have to fight if he needed to, not because he wanted to prove himself to people. He would know that home was his place as well as mine, a place he could come to and feel safe, wanted, and loved.

I would make sure I talked to my kids and never missed anything, even if it was a basketball game or something simple as cheerleading practice. I would talk to my child and not at him or her. Just thinking of all the things I wanted to do with my child made me emotional.

"What's wrong, babe?" Kash asked as he walked into the room, pulling his shirt off. He had a fresh cut and looked good as hell.

"Nothing, I was just watching the news. Seeing those kids killing each other made me think about all the things I would do as a parent to ensure my child took the right path in life, you know. I hope we do not fail our child," I admitted.

"Baby, we will not. As long as we keep our family first and make sure things that are meant to be handled at home are handled at home, we will be good. We will have to keep family out of certain business, yet be open to our son or daughter reaching out to our family for things he or she doesn't want to come to us about because it will happen. We cannot be mad or upset about it because, as we can clearly see, it takes a village." He wiped my tears away.

"What did you do today?" I asked, changing the subject.

"Man, shit, I did some light shopping for you. I took the list off the fridge and picked all that stuff up, so you don't have to. How did things go with Nakari? Did y'all talk? What's up with her?"

"No. She wasn't home, and she's not answering my calls. I called my auntie, and she told me she had talked to her yesterday. I'm going to let her be and allow her to reach out when she's ready. I just don't want her to feel like she's alone because she's not. I feel like when I needed everybody, they were always there for me. I'm trying to be there for her as well, but she won't let me," I explained as Kash stripped off his outside clothes.

"Sometimes you can't force people. When she is ready to talk to you, she will. If it makes you feel better, send her a motivational message every day or simply just let her know you are there for her. That way, she knows you are still there, even when she's pushing everyone away. She is grieving in her own way, and maybe she's dealing with some things she hasn't told you about. Y'all are best friends. Nakari ain't gon' be on this for too long," he said and kissed me on the lips.

"Okay," I replied before going back downstairs and draining my chicken to put the barbecue sauce on it.

Once that was done, I started my herb and butter rice and string beans. My phone rang, and I picked it up.

"Hello?" I placed the phone on speaker and set it on the counter.

"I am looking for an Amarie," a guy's voice came through the speaker.

Kash came into the room and gave me a concerned look but did not say anything. I shrugged to let him know I didn't know what was going on.

"This is she," I said.

"I'm Detective Marshall, and I was calling to inform you of the passing of your husband, DeJuan Gibbs." There was a pause, and I tried to gather my words but could not find any.

"When did this happen?" I asked. I mean, I couldn't stand the man, but I didn't want to see him dead.

"Late last night. I tried to stop past your house, but it looked abandoned. DeJuan was in a hotel room that caught fire. I do have someone I am questioning about this incident, as he was not alone in the room. However, the other person made it out alive. Our fire department is investigating, and we will have more information for you soon. I am sorry for your loss." He ended the call.

My phone beeped, and I clicked to answer for Natalie.

"Girl, did you hear?" she yelled.

"Yeah, they just called and let me know DeJuan died in a hotel fire," I said.

"Bitch, no fucking way! Nakari is down at the police station, being questioned about a fire where a guy died. She just called my mom."

My head started spinning, and my mouth went dry. There

was no way this was a coincidence. Getting up, I put my shoes on and rushed outside.

"Babe, we have to go see what's going on," I said just as my phone rang again.

I decided not to answer, but Kash did. He placed it on speaker, and the world seemed to stop as I listened to the call.

"Natalia, I swear I do not have no reason to lie. Ask Amarie. She wanted me to kill him," Nakari lied.

CHAPTER THREE
AMARIE

Hearing those words come from Nakari had me in shock. This bitch straight lied on me, and for what reason? I had not done anything to her, yet she boldly lied on me. The last I checked, we were supposed to be the best of friends. It was almost as if God was removing people from my life left and right. I had only thought about asking him to remove the people who were not for me from my life, and this happened. So, I was afraid to pray and actually ask him because I couldn't afford to lose anyone else.

"What?" Natalia yelled.

"Call her and ask her. It wasn't supposed to even happen like that," she continued her bullshit.

Natalia knew that girl was lying; she had to. The question, though, was why? Why did she have to lie on me or blame me for something she did? Why did she even want to see me down bad like that when I had been down bad my entire life? I was finally having my moment, and, at that moment, I realized the saying was completely true—more money, more problems. I was finally coming into money, and the people I wanted to share it with, who I felt had been there with me, were the ones turning on me.

I was slowly starting to think that no one could be trusted. First, my mom, then watching Kash and Capri's shit, and now my best friend, my cousin, the person I shared clothes with. When she pissed in the bed, I would change the sheets for her, so she wouldn't get in trouble. We never had a problem before, and now, all of a sudden, we were here. I would have never expected this kind of shit from Nakari.

The entire time, Kash stayed quiet, not uttering one word. I kept my phone mute, trying to decide if I wanted to speak up or just let her talk. When I went to touch the button, Kash grabbed my hand.

"It'll be easier if she thinks you don't know. She is going to tell everyone what she wants to tell them. I can hear in her voice that the girl is coming down off a high and is scared. The easiest thing for her to do is blame you because it will look good. You are trying to divorce him. He is a crackhead, and look who his parents are. It will be an easy lead for them to follow. What they don't know is that you have a team behind you, and I'm willing to do whatever needs to be done to ensure your safety and that you stay free. Now, what I will tell you is this is going to be a long, draining process. Please try to stay as calm as possible in all situations. You are carrying my baby, and I'll say fuck all this doing the right thing shit and get active if something happens to my child," Kash told me just as the phone hung up.

Natalia called me right back and let out a loud sigh.

"My sister has reached the bikini bottom in life. I am so sorry she's doing this to you. I know that girl was lying. What is so unbelievable to me is that the bitch was getting high and possibly fucking this man. I can't for the life of me understand that," Natalia stated.

"Shit, me either," I replied as the wheels spun in my head.

There really wasn't much for me to say. Any words I could think of were all stuck. I was flabbergasted as I opened my laptop to check my emails. If this were to make the news or even get in the way of my growing business, I would be defeated.

"I'm gon' call my mom and see if she can talk some sense into this girl. I love you, boo. No matter what, you keep that head up, bitch. Do not let that mufucka tilt because that crown may slip," she preached.

"Love you too." I quickly hung up the phone.

As much as I wanted to deal with the shit that was happening right now, I could not, and as much as I wanted to speak on it, the words would not form. I was growing tired of being on the shitty end of the stick.

Once I went through all my emails, I pulled up Safari and searched for lawyers. I didn't have much, but what I did have would go to them. I would even use the money Kash was giving me to ensure I had a good lawyer who would be paid in full.

"Ain't no need for all that. I already texted my lawyer. First thing Monday morning, we will go see her. Until then, don't discuss that shit." Kasha lifted my chin and kissed my lips.

Until that moment, I had forgotten he was in the room. I smiled at him. Hell, it was hard not to. Every time I felt like my back was against the wall, my man came out swinging for me. That's why, once we merged our companies, I would continue to treat his employees like they were mine and do right by him. I was going to make this man proud of me.

Kash rubbed his hands through my hair, massaging my scalp. Leaning my head back against his chest, I closed my eyes, enjoying the feeling.

"Okay," I replied just as my phone dinged.

Lifting it, I saw that my mother was texting me for an update about her money.

After reading her message twice, I powered my phone off, deciding to reply to her at another time. I needed to clear my head. With everything going on, I didn't even have time to be happy about having a child or to even talk to Kasha about if he really wanted this with me because it would quickly turn our one-year stand into eighteen years. Letting out a loud sigh, I grabbed his hands, making him stop rubbing my head.

"Kasha, I'm having a baby, and look what's going on. I am not supposed to be stressed. I don't even know if this is what you want." Standing up, I turned so we could be face to face.

"What do you mean? I would have told you to get rid of it already if I wasn't happy. I'm against that, though. Of course, I want this with you. I know this shit was supposed to be a one-year thing, and we have done so much in so little time. The year is almost up, and you've made a lot of progress. I know shit keeps getting hard for you, but as long as I can make it easier, I will," Kash told me.

Dropping my head, I let the tears fall. Shit was so hectic, and it seemed like every corner I turned or every step toward progress I made, there was some shit waiting to knock me down.

Kash placed his hand underneath my chin and lifted my head while his other hand slowly wiped away the tears that had fallen. Looking into Kash's eyes, I saw the love he had for me, and I hoped like hell he could see the love I had for him. Kash extended his left hand and placed it on my stomach. If the doctors hadn't said anything, I would never have known I was pregnant. Even with me having moments when I didn't feel well, being pregnant was the last thing on my mind. My stomach was still flat, making me wonder if I would become big and swollen or if I would stay small.

Kash bent down and placed his head in the crook of my neck. For a while, we stood there quietly.

In the middle of our little moment, Kash's phone started ringing. We both looked over, and I saw a random number on the screen. Kash picked up the phone and placed it on speaker.

"Hello."

"Listen, I'm on my way. The cops will be there shortly, and they have an arrest warrant. Tell her to stay calm and don't say anything until she speaks with me." The lady spoke quickly before the phone disconnected.

"Fuckkk!" Kash yelled, and then he pulled me back toward him. "Listen, the cops are on their way. They are going to arrest you. Please stay calm. We do not need your pressure to go up. Your lawyer is already on her way. Her name is Miranda Stewart. She will probably be at the station shortly after you get there. She can't meet you there because her husband probably let her know what was about to take place."

Sucking my teeth, I removed Kash's hands from my stomach and stepped away from him. Looking down at the floor, I did my best not to cry. Hell, crying was not getting me anywhere. I blinked my tears away as I walked over to the closet, grabbed a hoodie, and placed it on. I had heard it was cold inside that place, and I wanted to have as much warmth as I could. While I slowly moved around the room, Kash quickly threw on clothes and got whatever else he needed. I had not even prepared myself to be arrested, nor had the thought crossed my mind.

Hearing banging on the front door, my heart rate quickly sped up. As much as I wanted to pretend like I was not scared, I couldn't. My stomach was doing somersaults, and all of a sudden, the urge to take a poop came about.

"Relax, I got you. I'm going to get you out of there as quickly as I possibly can," Kash told me.

"Okay," I replied.

I tried to sound convincing, but hell, I didn't even sound convincing to my damn self, so I knew he didn't buy it.

"I'm going to open the door when you tell me to." Kash slowly walked to the door while keeping his eyes on me.

"Go 'head," I told him.

He unlocked the door and opened it. Cops came barging in with guns drawn.

"She's pregnant," he told the one lady police officer who rushed toward me.

It was like she didn't even care what he said as she knocked me to the ground. My hands immediately went to my stomach.

"Yo, she's fucking pregnant. Tell that bitch to chill, or I swear to God, I'm filing a fucking lawsuit against you. Let something happen to my wife or child." I could hear Kash yelling at the police officers.

"Show me your fucking hands!" she screamed.

"At least let me up. I'm not trying to do anything. I'm pregnant. Please get off me!" I cried as the lady police officer kept her knee on my back.

"On my mama, if this bitch doesn't get off my wife, y'all gon' be doing more than making an arrest in this bitch!" Kash screamed.

I heard the officers quickly telling him to calm down.

"Let her up, Gibbs." The male officer pulled the lady off me, and I swear I wanted to beat her ass.

Once they let me up, Kash calmed down. The lady forced my hands behind my back and cuffed me while reading me my Miranda rights. Then they roughly pulled me off the ground and led me to the back of the cop car. Once inside, I began to bawl. I was scared as hell, and as tears fell down my face, I only could imagine what was in the back of this paddy wagon or going on outside of it.

The car pulled off, and I swear we hit every bump on the road the way I was bouncing around. I was now afraid for my child and what could happen while I was back there. No one had made sure I was buckled in, and with my hands behind my back, I couldn't stop myself from sliding all over the place. Feeling the car come to a complete stop and not move for a while, my anxiety grew. I didn't know where I was or if they planned to get me out anytime soon.

The drive felt like hours, but it was probably only fifteen minutes.

When they opened the doors, I was a little relieved. They walked me into the place and stopped me against the wall, where they gave me a yellow wristband with my name on it. Then, they took my shoestrings and the strings out of my hoodie. Finally, I was patted down before they led me into a room.

"Detectives will be in here shortly to speak with you," the police officer told me and closed the door, leaving me alone.

CHAPTER FOUR

KASH

I could still hear Terrell's words before I shot him. Every so often, I would think about how he made this gurgling noise, and then his body slumped over. The images of Carmen flying off that swing would play in my head again. She was the very reason I had a hard time actually having to kill people. I hated the sight of someone bleeding out, and watching it reminded me of her sometimes. Seeing her lifeless with no help and nothing anyone could do pained me. My phone ringing brought me out of my thoughts, and I quickly answered.

"Yo?"

"Man, where you at? I just swung by the crib, and you weren't there," Von said.

"I'm on my way to the police station. Some shit happened with Amarie and that Nakari situation," I replied, keeping it brief.

"Get back with me when you leave that jawn or if you need anything. You know I ain't stepping foot near there or in there," he told me.

"Heard you." I hung up the phone and continued to speed through traffic.

Pulling into the parking lot of the precinct, I parked my car and all but ran inside the building. I walked to the window and waited until someone decided to greet me. After standing there for about ten minutes, I decided to take a seat. As much as I wanted to show my ass, I knew it would do Amarie no good. My lawyer was good, so I knew that if anything, I would be able to bail Amarie out, and I refused to leave until they allowed me to do so. I hated that she was in a situation like this, all over her bitch ass cousin. I was tempted to have someone kill her ass, but I knew that would hurt their family, and I was not trying to do that. Plus, I figured it would bring more heat to Amarie.

"Excuse me, did you need any help?" A lady had finally come to the window.

Standing, I walked over to the window. This lady was pretty as hell, and she looked good in her little police uniform. However, the way she chewed on her gum and seemed to have an attitude for no reason had me frowning at her.

"Yeah, they brought my wife in here, and I'm trying to see what's going on with her."

"What's her name and date of birth?" she asked, and I gave her the information she needed.

I watched as she typed it into the computer while loudly popping her gum.

"She's only been processed. That will allow her a phone call, and maybe she will call you," was all she gave me.

"Okay, anything else I need to know?" I seemed to have a lot of questions lately, and none were really being answered.

"Nope." She walked off.

Pinching the bridge of my nose, I walked out of the precinct and to my car. I knew my lawyer was somewhere around there, and I was going to wait in the parking lot until I saw her. While waiting, I checked my emails. There were a few in Amarie's box, and I checked those, too, since she had her email on my laptop. I smiled when I saw that the people who were renting from her had paid their rent on the app that I made for her. She also had a few emails about the house she wanted to purchase. I responded to them, not wanting her to miss the opportunity.

Once I was done, I closed my laptop, set it on the passenger seat, and reclined my chair while watching the door. This shit was stressful. However, I would not want to be any other place than there, making sure my bitch was cool. Seeing Miranda walk out of the police station, I hopped out of my car and walked over to her. I knew I scared her ass because she clutched her chest like she was clutching her pearls and dropped her phone.

"Shit, Kasha. What is wrong with you?" She picked her phone up off the ground.

Keeping quiet, I waited for her to tell me what was going on.

"She hasn't seen the judge yet, which is when she will be able to get bail. They ain't gon' budge on the release on her own recognizance simply because of the charges she may be facing. Now, from talking to her, she did not really have much information to give. I will have to go down to the courts on Monday and get their paperwork to see exactly what they have on her and what evidence they have. From my standpoint, they will not go easy on her. This guy who died, his parents are very well known in the courts, and I am sure they are pressing the issue, which is why the police are moving this way. I know for a fact that she's not seeing a judge today. It's the weekend, so you know how that goes." She spoke calmly but fast.

"I know. She ain't built for jail, and she's pregnant. I am not worried about the bond. We cool on the money. As soon as they give her one or you hear anything, let me know. I'm going to talk with her family. It is her cousin that's blaming her for this shit. So, I want to see what they heard."

"That's what she told me. She said the man was her husband. Basically, that will be good for the opposition. He's dead, the cousin is blaming her, and from what Amarie said, the two were pretty close, which is another thing they could bring up. She will have to go through a hell of a process. I'm not going to lie; this is going to be a tough one, especially if this goes in front of a jury, which I will push for. I'll have to put her on the stand. Judging by the way she acted, she's either innocent or her ass deserves an Oscar," Miranda voiced, saying some shit I was already thinking.

"Okay, so basically, we about to play a crazy waiting game, and then it gets even crazier. I am paying you to do your best, so get ready to put up one hell of a fight. I also want you to view the footage from my home. The way the one lady police officer handled Amarie was crazy. I need you to go back in there and see if they can have the baby checked. Amarie was on the ground, and the bitch had her knee in her back, even after we told her she was pregnant. The baby needs to be checked." Placing my hands in my pocket, I walked to my car, feeling defeated.

I was leaving, my girl was not leaving with me, and it wasn't shit I could do. Getting in my car, I started it and pulled off, driving toward Natalia's house. When shit happened, they always met up at someone's house, and I knew it was not Nakari's. The entire drive, I tried to gather my thoughts because if they said anything out of pocket, I was going to snap. And if anyone had a problem, we would have to handle it how they saw fit.

I pulled into Natalia's driveway and slowly got out, wishing I had stopped to grab a bottle 'cause a nigga was stressed. I took the steps two at a time and banged on the door like the police were just doing to my door a few minutes ago.

"Natalia, this bet not be one of them niggas you used to be fucking, or we gon' be smoking on that nigga," Von barked on the other side of the door.

After hearing the locks undo, the door quickly swung open, and this nigga was standing there in pajamas, mean-mugging me. Pushing past him, I walked into the house, and just like I thought, everyone was sitting around, looking just as stressed as I was.

"What we got to do?" Natalia asked.

"Wait. I had my lawyer go up there, and she said his family is putting pressure on them. Amarie ain't seen a judge yet, but that is expected since it's the weekend. Nakari basically fed them all this bullshit that will be good for the prosecutors when it's time to take Amarie to court. Miranda is going to get all the files, so she can see what they have on her. She didn't tell me what any of her charges were, and I didn't even think to ask her. I did tell her that if they give her a bond to let me know. ROR is out of the window, simply based on the fact that a man was killed," I explained to them.

"God, where did I go wrong with my child?" Auntie said with a cigarette between her long fingers that displayed long red nails and henna.

"I was trying to figure that out too. You raised a hoe and a liar. That's crazy, Ma," Von spoke, causing everyone to laugh.

I was surprised to see Amarie's mom and dad there.

"So, basically, my child may do time because her favorite cousin wanted to razzle and dazzle with that white girl and a used to be blue-collar nigga," her daddy snapped.

"Listen, not too much to my child. She fucked up. I get it. She's wrong, dead ass wrong, but it's still my daughter." Auntie stood, defending Nakari.

"But where's the lie in what he said? That is not fair to Amarie. Nakari fucked up really bad, and she's placing other people's lives in jeopardy. We all know that Amarie ain't capable of no shit like that, and she shouldn't have to suffer because Nakari made a mistake. We need to get her some help and make sure she gets cleaned up off that shit," Natalia spoke up.

"That's all understandable. We fuck up as people, and I'm not justifying what she did because we all know Amarie shouldn't be a part of that shit. Amarie is my child too, and she's not wrong for feeling however she feels, but y'all ain't 'bout to bad mouth my daughter," Auntie fussed.

"I'm going keep my mouth shut then because if we're being honest, that girl ain't shit. For her to do some shit like that, it had to be them drugs playing tricks in her head. But I'm gon' shut up, though, because that's your daughter." Von took a sip of his drink.

I could tell just by that gesture that his ass had been hanging around Natalia too much because that was shit she did all the time.

"I'm gon' go ahead and head out. Kasha, if she needs anything or you need anything, let me know. Please keep me posted. I'm gon' talk to Nakari and see if I can get her to put an end to all this shit because she needs to own up to her shit." Auntie slammed the door on her way out.

"That bitch needs to get her daughter because she is fucking with my money. Kasha, did she leave a check or anything? That's what I came for," this lady had the nerve to ask.

Von jumped out of his seat and hauled ass to the door. "Aye, Ma. This nappy wig, big back bitch just called you a bitch and said if you ain't get your daughter to change her statement so she can get her money, it's gon' be some chairs moving and ass whippings," he called out.

"Oh, the bitch wants some smoke with me, son? Hold my weed and hair." Auntie came rushing back through the door with her stocking cap thingy on. She kicked off her flip-flops and removed her hoops so fast.

"Natalia, get your mammy before I disrespect your house."

"Ma, I heard her say that shit too," Natalia lied.

That was all it took for this lady to start hollering for her to get up and throw her dukes up.

"I ain't about to be no bitch, like I ain't got a military background." Amarie's mom stood and tried to run up, but she slipped.

I don't know how or what she slipped on, but the way she went down was hilarious.

"That was God, bitch. You know I'm God's child, and he don't play 'bout me. Give me my damn hair and weed. Smoking up all my shit. This ole linebacker-ass bitch beating herself up. I don't even know why the old whore is here."

Everyone was dying with laughter. Even though it was not the right time, I felt like we all needed that laugh.

CHAPTER FIVE
AMARIE

I felt dirty as hell sitting inside that cage like an animal. The police officers questioned me for so long, and I just didn't have the answers they were looking for.

"You know we are going to keep you here. You are going to have that baby in prison, and we will just take him and place him. You can't raise that baby in jail," I remember them saying like I was going to give them some information I had been holding.

I was in a holding cell, and the only thing they kept giving me was bologna sandwiches and water. I kept throwing up every time I ate the sandwich, and the water was not enough. They gave me more tissue than food. I watched as multiple females came and left. Some were even switched to a different place, and I wished they would do the same for me.

"Excuse me," I called from the cell.

Although I was sitting down, I felt dizzy. My head was spinning, and my stomach hurt. I knew I needed some kind of food or fresh air or something.

"Please help me," I said to a man who walked by.

He just looked at me and kept going.

Bending over, I threw up the bread I had eaten. I figured the meat on the sandwich was no good. My head pounded as I slid down the wall and wiped the sweat from my forehead. I felt like I was about to die, and no one cared. Laying my head back against the dirty gate of the cell, which was cold, I closed my eyes. I wanted to say a prayer, but I done prayed to God so many times in the past two days, so I knew he ain't hear me.

"Ma'am, you okay?" I heard.

Lifting my head, I looked at a lady police officer who was squatted down, so she could be at eye level with me.

"No. I'm pregnant, and those sandwiches are not staying down. I'm dizzy and hot. I do not feel good at all. Do y'all have a nurse or something? I need the hospital," I lowly said.

I didn't even bother to lift my head off the gate. I needed the coldness it provided to my body. Leaning over, I threw up until I was dry heaving. There was nothing left inside me. Wrapping my arms around my knees and pulling them up to my chest, I placed my head down.

"That's not good. I'm going to see if we can have some officers transport you to the nearest hospital. You may need fluids and food. Hang tight for me." She stood to her feet and walked off.

The unknown was killing me as I waited. I didn't know if they were going to keep me there, if I would go to the hospital, if they would bring me something else to eat, or what. The only thing I knew was, I hated Nakari for this, and I never wanted to speak to her again in life. I didn't even care why she did what she did; it had caused me harm. Being as far away from her as possible after all this was cleared up would be the best thing for me. And if that meant cutting my auntie off and my cousin, then that's what would be done. I loved them wholeheartedly. However, I could not accept what she had done to me, and whatever reason she had for doing it was between her, God, and DeJuan. She would have to deal with the karma for what she had done to me. I was no longer even trying to say her name or hear it.

"She looks fine to me. If her ass can't keep down a sandwich, give her something else. She committed a crime, and that is why she's here. This criminal does not get any special privileges. She's going to jail, and when she makes it, that's when she can decide what she eats and what she doesn't," the lady police officer who arrested me said.

"She's fucking pregnant," the other lady snapped.

I took the time to read their badges. I kept repeating their badge numbers and names in my head until I had committed them to memory.

"Okay, congratulations. You packed lunch, right? Give it to her, and while you're at it, give her some Pepsi and whatever else she wants to cry about. She wasn't crying when she was out there setting people up, was she?" the lady whose badge said Hanks snapped back.

"You don't have to be like that all the time. What happened to innocent until proven guilty? For goodness' sake, look at her. She doesn't even look good. If anything happens to her while I am on the clock, I will feel bad. She needs medical attention and now. This is not the kind of heat you want to bring to this jail. Allow her medical attention, and when she gets that, she will be brought back here or up state road. Whichever it is, you know her and her child will be in good condition," Tristian argued.

"You think I give a damn about a criminal's life? Especially one who took the life of someone else." She raised her voice a little.

The entire time they argued back and forth, I felt myself

getting weaker. The last thing I remembered was my head feeling heavy and everything going black.

———

Hearing a rapid thump caused me to open my eyes and look around. When I noticed the white walls and looked over at the machines, I realized I was in the hospital. Trying to sit up at the sound of Kash's voice, I noticed my hand was cuffed to the bed like I would try to escape, which would be dumb on my part.

"Fuck what y'all talking 'bout. Lock me up, then. My fucking wife and baby laid up in that bitch, and you trying to hold me back. Cuff me. Fuck you mean?" Kash yelled.

"I'm okay, babe. I feel better," I yelled so he would calm down.

Kash was still trying to push past the officer and security guard who were blocking him from entering the room. The security guard took it a step further and grabbed Kash's arm. The two quickly began to tussle while the police officer sat back and watched.

"You want to show your ass, huh?" the security guard barked.

Kash quickly threw a punch and followed it with another one, which landed somewhere on the guard's side, that put him down. The way he grabbed his side when he hit the ground and balled up, I knew it hurt.

The police officer pushed himself off the wall and went to grab Kash. My man quickly stepped back, pulled his pants up, and got ready for the police officer to swing.

"Come on. Do you really want to go down for assault on a cop?" the police officer tried to reason.

I guess after those two punches the security guard got, the police officer didn't want any parts, and I didn't blame him.

Kash sucked his teeth but dropped his hands. His ass was not trying to go to jail, and I did not want him to. I didn't know his next move. However, I was happy to see him. I could smell his Dior Sauvage cologne in the room, and he was not even in there. Just the smell of him made me wet between my legs, yet I could not have him how I wanted him.

"Ma, you good? My baby cool? Are you hurt? Did they hurt you?" Kash fired question after question.

"Yes, please calm down. It's already enough with me being here," I told him.

The moment I heard my auntie yelling, I knew all hell was about to break loose again. The security guard was now in the seat, not saying anything, and the police officer looked like he was ready to lock everybody up. My auntie was doing the most, and they still would not let her in the room. At that point, I didn't even see why they were letting them in the back.

"Ms., you have to take a seat. The doctors will be out to talk to you all, but she is still in police custody, so no one is able to come in and out of the room except the people who need to. If y'all have anyone else coming up here, please explain that to them. I have already dealt with enough from this man and won't tolerate too much more. All your asses will be in jail if y'all keep this up. You gon' fuck around and find out that you are doing too much," the officer expressed. He was fed up, and Kash's ass did not even move.

The officer kindly pulled the door to the room, so it would be basically closed. There was a little crack in the door, and the curtain was not all the way closed. I felt like I had no privacy. However, being laid up in that bed with a blanket and fluids felt better than being in that cold ass cell.

"At least let me give her this food or something. Y'all ain't been feeding her right. She's carrying a baby, and them little waters and sandwiches ain't feed my ass, so I know she hungry!" my auntie called out, and I laughed.

There was no reason for them to be up there acting a fool. If anything, that would probably make it worse for me since I knew there was no way in hell they would let me out of there.

A doctor came into the room with a small smile on her face.

"Can you tell me what's going on with my baby? I know the security guard and the cop out there couldn't," I said to her as she looked at the monitors.

"Everything with the baby is okay. It is you I'm worried about. Your blood pressure was extremely high when you came in, and that can not only cause a great deal of problems, not only for you but for the baby as well. I also have a scale being brought in, so we can measure your weight. You are dehydrated, which is why you are on fluids. In the position you're in, I will have to see what they can do for you as far as vitamins and making sure you stay hydrated. Until your pressure is down, I will keep you here. I need to check your vitals again, and a nurse should be in shortly to weigh you and all those things since you were out cold when you came in. I will also have a talk with your husband, who I hear has been causing problems because he is so worried about you. I'll have that talk with him after I have all the information I need," she stated while getting her things ready.

A light tap on the door made us both look up, and a nurse came in with a little machine.

"Oh, perfect. You can take her weight while I'm in here, so I can just put it in her chart." The doctor smiled while the nurse sanitized her hands.

The police officer came in and uncuffed me from the bed.

He quickly walked out before I stood and stepped on the scale. Looking down, I sighed. I had gone from a cute one hundred and seventy something pounds to one hundred and sixty-two. The doctor looked at it and then started typing on the computer.

"You should be gaining weight, not losing it. Is there anything we can help you with?" she asked.

"No. All this stuff that's going on is just getting to me," I admitted.

There was no way I lost that much weight in a matter of days, so I knew this was the effect of everything going on around me.

"You have to get it together if you want this baby to survive. You already have a lot going on. Things that seem to be out of your control and the things you can control. You need to make the best of them, even this situation. Your baby deserves that much. I have watched so many young moms stress themselves and run up their blood pressure, and they never got it until it was too late. Don't let that be you," she said, giving me a lot to think about.

I wanted the best for my baby and myself, but the way things were looking, I wasn't sure if I was capable of providing that.

CHAPTER SIX

AMARIE

A s I put my clothes back on, I wanted to cry. I was finally discharged from the hospital, and my baby was okay, but I had to return to jail instead of heading home like I wanted to. I moved as slowly as possible and wished like hell they had taken their time with my discharge papers like they usually did, but that did not happen.

"Take care, and make sure you do your best to keep the baby as healthy as possible," the doctor said while handing me my paperwork.

The moment she walked out the door, the female officer who was watching me today came in with a wheelchair. She instructed me to sit down before she cuffed my hands and feet and placed a blanket over me. I was thankful they made things a little discreet, but I still kept my head down as we made our way out of the hospital. A lot of people were staring, but nobody pulled out their phones, for which I was thankful. Once we were outside, they helped me into the back of the police car and strapped me in before climbing in themselves and pulling off.

"You're going to go in and see the judge since he is seeing people," the lady told me.

"Okay," I replied as my stomach began to bubble.

They helped me out of the car once we made it back, and we walked inside. My movements were slow because my feet were still cuffed until we were back inside. They checked me again like I was not just cuffed to a hospital bed with no visitors. We made it down a long hallway, and I was placed in line with people who were going in to see the judge.

When it was my turn, I stepped into the room in front of the screens and stated my name and date of birth. The judge told me how serious my charges were and the allegations against me. He also let me know that because of that, the release on my own recognizance that I could have received was not an option, which Miranda had already prepared me for.

"Bail is two hundred thousand dollars." He slammed his gavel, and I was escorted out and led right to a phone.

I only knew Natalia's number by heart, so that is who I called.

"Instead of screaming free the guys, I'm screaming free the girls. Are you okay, love?" she asked, and I instantly smiled.

"I'm alive. That's all that matters. I need you to call Kash for me right fast. I got about two minutes on this phone before the next girl comes out," I quickly spoke.

"Okay." I heard her press a few buttons before the line went silent.

"What's up?" Kash's voice came through the phone.

"My bail is two hundred thousand. That's a lot of money. Can you just make sure you keep money on my books and pick up the phone when I call? I'm not asking y'all to come get me. That's a lot." I sighed.

"I'm on my way," he said, and the line went silent again.

"He hung up. I love you, and whatever you need, just let me know," Natalia said before I had to hang up.

Wiping the tears that fell from my eyes, I went and stood behind the girl who was in front of me when I first got in line. We were now on the opposite wall, waiting for everyone to finish. I could tell by the faces and how we were being separated who was going home and who was going to jail. A lot of females were smiling and talking shit while others were sobbing. The girl in front of me turned around and looked at me before she did a little giggle.

I had to turn around and see who she was looking at and what was funny. When I didn't see anything, I began to stare her down, hoping she said something out of line to me. Instead of holding my stare, she turned back around and looked ahead of us. Placing my foot on the wall, I watched as everyone came and went until there were no more. We were placed back in our cells while the people who I assumed had the ROR went home.

This time, when I went inside the cell, it wasn't the same one, and three other girls were in there with me. We all looked the same—sad and lost—except one who looked like she was happy to be there. I could only imagine what life had to be like on the outside for her if she was happy to be in there.

"Amarie." I heard my name called, and I quickly stood from my seat on the bench and went to the gate.

It was opened, and they cuffed my hands before letting me out and leading me back up to the front. I just knew the judge had changed his mind because the bail he gave me was ridiculously high.

"Stay out of here," Tristian said as she uncuffed me. I will never forget her or her name.

"I will. And thank you." I smiled at her.

When I walked outside with my paperwork, I spotted

Kash's car. That man had come to get me. He stepped out of
the car, and I ran over to jump in his arms. He carried me all
the way to the car, keeping his arms wrapped tightly
around me.

"I missed you so much, baby!" I cried into the crook of his
neck.

"I told you as soon as they gave you bail, I was coming to
get you. We are going to make that little money back. What
matters is you being home to help me." He placed me on my
feet and opened the car door for me.

I climbed inside before reaching over and opening his door.
He got in and pulled off. I never wanted to come back to that
place, and everything I had on was going in the trash. Instead
of going back to Kash's old house, we went to the new house,
and I smiled. Hell, if I was honest, I really didn't want to go
back to the old house ever again.

I was fine with living in the new place. We agreed that we
would wait until my marriage was over and the baby came
before we moved into the new house, but shit changed, and
that would be one of the things that changed under my
control. The moment the car stopped, I headed into the house
and right to the bathroom, where I stripped off my clothes and
threw them in the trash.

We had moved some stuff in there, so I was not too concerned
about not having any clothes. The water hit my body, and it felt
so good. I washed days' worth of filth off me. I scrubbed my entire
body, hair and all, a few times before stepping out and wrapping
a towel around me. Taking a seat in front of the big mirror in the
bathroom, I used the blow dryer that was on the shelf to dry my
hair. It was now a big fro, and I did not care.

Walking into the bedroom, I climbed on the bed, allowing
my body to relax and sink into the mattress. Being inside that

place for that small amount of time made me realize how much shit we took for granted.

Kash climbed into bed, got between my legs, and kissed my lips. I immediately wrapped my legs around him and stuck my tongue in his mouth, deepening the kiss. Kash kissed down my body before spreading my legs and coming face to face with my kitty. I looked down at him and watched as he just stared at her for a second. I had shaved while I was in the shower, so I wasn't worried about too much hair being down there. He licked his lips and then blew on my clit, causing my body to shiver. This man held my ankles while he leaned in and went to work on me. He licked and sucked on my clit like it was his favorite meal.

"Damn," I moaned.

The shit felt so good. I leaned my head back and chewed on my bottom lip as he slid a finger inside me and worked my middle. Being the team player I was, I grabbed my legs and held them apart while he French kissed my pussy.

"Hmmm." I dropped my legs as my body shook.

"Nah, beautiful, put them bitches back up. You are stopping me from eating, and you know I don't like that," he said in a thick, husky voice that sent chills through me.

Then, he bent back down and sucked my clit into his mouth, holding it there while he swirled his tongue around it. Kash flipped us over so I was sitting on his face. I slowly rocked my hips against his tongue until he tapped my leg and motioned for me to turn around. Just like the good girl I was, I did as told.

While I sat on his face, his dick stood straight up. The sight of it caused my mouth to water, so I did the only logical thing. Grabbing him in my small hands, I spit on the tip before working my hands in a circular motion. Kash had somehow reached underneath me and was rubbing my clit while he ate my ass.

"Ohh, daddy," I moaned on his dick.

In my mind, we were in competition, so I slowly sucked the head into my mouth before going all the way down, making sure to gag, so I could gather more spit. I repeated that a few times until his dick and my hands were covered in spit. Then, I started using my hands to jerk him off while I sucked the rest of him. I bobbed my head and moved my hands at the same rhythm while he had his thumb in my ass and sucked on my clit.

My body shook as I came all over Kash's face. My body stiffened, and all he did was lift me off him. I lay on my back, trying to catch my breath as Kash eased up my body, rubbing his dick back and forth against my clit. He had my legs spread apart like a V as he entered me. He slid in and out of me so slowly, making sure to dig deep.

"Fuck, this shit is so wet." He groaned as he pulled out of me and then slammed back into me.

"Give me my dick, please," I begged, not wanting him to go slow. I needed to be fucked like only he fucked me.

"Say less." Kash leaned down and placed my legs on his shoulders.

I heard the sound of my rose toy before I felt it on my clit. Kasha held it there while he stuffed me with dick.

"Arghh fuck!" I screamed, trying to scoot back.

"Nah, stay there. I been wanting to try this since you got this bitch," he said as he fucked me harder.

My body began to jerk, and I tried to cover my mouth because I was bound to scream.

Kasha knocked my hand down.

"Let me hear that shit. Ain't nobody here, so be as loud as

you want. Damn, bae. That's right. Cream on my shit." Kash groaned as my body locked up.

I had never experienced something that felt so good, and even with me locking up, that man was still pumping inside me. He twisted my body sideways, giving me a break for a second before he held onto my legs and slid back inside me. One leg was underneath him, while the other was on his shoulder. He placed the rose back on my clit and began to give me long, deep strokes. Kash let my leg go and let it just rest on his shoulder while he slid his thumb into my ass.

"Ohhhh, fuck. Baby, please!" I cried.

This man found his angle and began to repeatedly hit the same spot that caused my body to lock up again. This time, I heard the fluids leave my body. It sounded like I was peeing, but I didn't have to pee. Kash only held my leg tighter and fucked me harder until his dick slipped out. I swear, all I could do was scream until my eyes rolled, and I felt like I couldn't breathe.

"Damn, baby, squirt on this dick," Kash coached.

He took the rose off me for a second before telling me to flip over, which I did, and tooted my ass in the air.

My body shook as he slid back inside me. I guess he had ditched the rose because it was now next to my head, still vibrating. Not wanting any more of that, I knocked it off the bed. Kash slid inside me and tightly gripped my waist. I threw my ass back on him, causing us both to moan. He slid his finger back into my ass and moved it around while he fucked me. Then he slapped my ass and gripped my butt cheeks before he pulled out of me and licked from the crack of my ass down to my dripping wet box.

Once my body started shaking, he stood and slid back inside me. My body fell flat on the bed, and he fell with me. He wrapped his legs over mine, grabbing a hand full of my hair.

"I fucking love you. You hear me? It will always be us against the world. Whatever you want, it's yours. This pussy so good, I'm willing to die 'bout it, and it ain't much I'm willing to die 'bout." He groaned in my ear.

"Daddy, fuck!" I screamed.

"You hear me, baby? We locked in forever. Fuck that year," he said as he pumped harder and harder.

Our moans grew louder as he shot his load inside me. My man said it was forever, so shit was forever with us. Closing my eyes, I fell asleep with his dick still inside me.

CHAPTER SEVEN

VON

I drove double the speed limit to my warehouse. My entire team was there and waiting for my arrival. To say I was pissed was an understatement. For the first time in my life, my trap house had been raided. The good thing was, there wasn't shit in that house but a few pounds of weed. The house next door that I had the crack in was left untouched. However, I knew we would have to close the shop and relocate. I was gon' move everything out and have Kash put them bitches on the market for me in a month or so. What got me was that the shit was in a good neighborhood, so I knew someone had to have fucked up.

I had been using this same house since I made the decision to move smarter and not just on the streets, so for it to take a hit meant that shit was going wrong. The one thing I was happy about was that the two people in the house were solid, and I knew there was no way they would snitch, so my operation was safe. As long as they were down, I would make sure their families were cool and their books were full. That was the least I could do on my end.

I drove around the block two times before parking in the lot to make sure no one was followed by the cops, and there wasn't any suspicious activity. Once I was sure the coast was clear, I parked and climbed out, locking the door behind me.

When I walked inside the building, I dapped up the security working the door and dismissed the naked bitches who were cooking up the work.

"Y'all done for the day. Collect y'all full day's pay on the way out." I made sure to pay them bitches every day. In case an emergency came up, they would always have some bread in their pockets.

I waited for all the females to leave; I didn't discuss any business in front of females because, in my eyes, they could be the most disloyal. All they needed was a nigga like me to give them good dick and broken promises for them to tell, and I was not having it. The only thing they knew was this place, and no one could just get in.

"Anybody want to explain to me what the fuck went down?" I asked, clenching my jaws.

The door to the warehouse swung open, and Big Red walked in, holding one of my young workers, Feek, by the back of his hoodie like the child he was. Feek was twenty and fresh out of high school. He had started school late and then failed, which made shit for him look bad. It did not help that his dad and mom didn't give a fuck about him. Feek was a bad ass, dirty little boy, who I gave an opportunity, so to see Big Red with him gripped up had me looking at him sideways.

"He might got some information for you. I was watching the houses for you and saw his ass getting out the back of a twelve car. He had the nerve to have his hood on and his head down. I made him strip already. He ain't have shit on him or no wires. That's why he's back in his clothes. I ain't feel too comfortable having a man butt ass naked in my front seat at gunpoint, or else I would have brought him with no clothes," Big Red informed me.

Again, I was quiet, letting what he said sink in. I was trying to process the shit, but my trigger finger was itching like a muthafucka. Just as I opened my mouth to speak, the doors to the warehouse opened. I was not afraid of it being the cops as they would have had to do more than use a fingerprint to access this bitch without me or security, and security was right next to me.

"Fuck Feek do?" Kash asked.

I knew his ass was stressed because he was smoking and had a big ass Backwood neatly rolled and tucked behind his ear. That man ain't even walk around like that. I had been doing so well with not having to kill my soldiers, but right now, I was ready to go against everything I stood for and take this nigga out because he was a liability. I hated that it was him because he was so young with a future that he just went ahead and fucked up.

"Look, I ain't gon' lie like I wasn't in that car because I was. My ass got booked with a brick on me, and they offered to let me out if I gave them you. I knew I fucked up because they came over the speaker asking did they take us all in. They even let me keep the brick, which was how my money never came up short," he explained.

"You telling me you was ready to get me knocked over you fucking up and getting caught with a brick?" I snapped. I could feel my voice rising each time I said something.

Feek's uncle looked disappointed in him. He was the sole reason I even let Feek get down with us. I fucked with Dell and knew he would never vouch for this kind of shit. I had been moving smart my whole life and staying under the radar. Now, because his ass fucked up, he was trying to take everyone with him, and I wasn't going to let that happen.

"What the fuck was I supposed to do? I'm not built for jail!" Feek yelled like that was supposed to justify his actions.

"You should have never entered a man's world, then. You know the risks of this shit and more than likely, if you afraid of jail, you was gon' end up dead or move smart enough to stack and go legit. You do not fucking tell, under any circumstances. You take that shit like a man. You fucked up. You stand on that shit. You don't sell the next person out. The person that's feeding your family. He makes sure we all eat," Dell roared.

Feek went to open his mouth and say something else but caught the surprise of his life. Hell, we all did.

Pew Pew.

The two gunshots had me ducking to get out of the way because I didn't know where the shit came from. Pulling my own gun from my waist, I quickly turned my body, only to see Kash standing there with his gun still aimed. Not only did he shoot Feek, but his ass shot Dell too. Both of them lay on the ground with blood pouring from their heads.

"Who the fuck next? Huh? This what muthafuckas wanted, right? Y'all wanted my brother to have a nigga next to him who he ain't have to question?" Kash snapped, and I was shocked.

Everything was happening so fast. The anger I saw on his face was something to remember, and I knew this moment did not just bring that on. I always told Kash he was too calm, and that was never good for a person. Because once that demon inside them woke up, there was no telling what they would do. I no longer saw the look in him that he had after he killed Terrell. He now had the look of a straight killer. His eyes were pitch black, and he looked like a lost soul.

"Well, that's handled. I'm gon' need everyone to lay low and wait for my call. Toss the burner phones y'all have, and we gon' get new ones. There's no telling what he told them, so I have to switch things up. Just bear with me," I instructed my team and ended the meeting.

Big Red had already started cleaning up the bodies with the help of a few of my cleaners. Kash and I headed outside to our cars. By then, he was already smoking again.

"You know I ain't need you to do that shit back there, right?" I asked after we had stood there for a few minutes, completely silent.

Kash was so zoned out that he didn't even bother sharing the weed.

"I know, nigga, but I did. Dell was cool and all, but that's his folks. I ain't need you having no back door shit, so he had to go to," he stated too calmly for my liking.

This was not Kash, and I didn't want him to become this person. He had accomplished too much and come way too far in life to be on some killer shit. Now, I wasn't knocking it if he had to, but this was one of the times he didn't have to. I couldn't even blame him for killing Dell because I didn't care what Kash did; if somebody killed him, I would go the distance to make sure they were dead. Right or wrong, he was my brother first.

"You been doing this shit for too long. I've watched you make moves, so you can run your shit the right way. That man ain't deserve to snake you again. I was serious about shit in there. I'm so tired of people playing with me, bro. I be giving people pass after pass. That billion-dollar business got people fooled because I'd rather rumble and get money than grab a gun. Nobody been hearing me since I was younger. It always took me going to extremes for niggas to understand that I am not to be played with. Everybody wants to play with me and my bitch, and I'm not no sucka, bro, or am I acting like one? Let me know. Do I seem pussy to you? 'Cause I ain't, so I'm gon' make people feel my wrath, the cops and whoever at this point. I'm tired, bro." Kash paced back and forth, and I felt for him, but I didn't know what to do.

I was one of those people who handled shit just like he just did. I would rather end the beef right away than go to war. Kash and I had always been complete opposites, and that is why we didn't clash. He did him, and I did me. We didn't even like the same kind of bitches or ways to get money. I would always choose the streets. I loved the feeling of fast money and the risk that came with it. I loved that everybody feared me, and if they didn't, they knew not to play with me.

Bitches flocked to me because not only did I look good, but I also had money and a whole lot of street cred. My name was good in every hood. I wasn't worried about no problems, and I liked shit that way. On the other hand, my boy chose to go the right way, and everyone knew that. I could fight, but I knew for a fact that I wasn't beating Kash, and I said that with pride. Just like I knew Kash didn't have the heart I did when it came to laying niggas down. I respected him for that because he never portrayed that he was like that.

"Bro, you good. You doing shit right. Nothing you have going on can be snatched from you because you doing it the right way. Keep that in the forefront. I know you got my back, and you ain't got to prove that shit. Yeah, people play with you, but that's 'cause you don't put them on they ass the first time they do it. But that's another thing that has gotten you to the level you are. Whatever you going through, handle that shit because this ain't it. You not 'bout to get your hands dirty. That is my job. You keep doing shit the right way because one day, in like thirty years, I'm gon' leave this shit alone, and I'm gon' need your help," I told him.

Kash nodded before he dapped me up, and we went our separate ways. I climbed into my car and waited for him to pull off before I went the opposite way to Natalia's house. I rode with the music playing low, and after a long, twenty-minute drive, I parked and got out of my car. Her crazy ass was sitting on the steps with her hair tied, smoking.

"Fuck you doing out here looking like you about to fight?" I questioned her.

"'Cause Kimmy 'bout to pull up." She handed me my personal phone, which I didn't even peep that I left behind.

As soon as the phone was in my hand, it began to vibrate. Kimmy's name came across the screen, and Natalia looked at me. Pressing the button, I ended the call, which sent Natalia haywire.

"Nah, pick up for the bitch. I already did. You was supposed to cut these bitches off, yet you still giving them the time of day. If you want to do you, go 'head, 'cause you know it's nothing for me to get back in the streets." She pointed her finger in my face.

"Try me," was all I said as I stepped past her and went into the house.

If her ass wanted to fight, that was on her. I planned to take a shower and take my ass to bed, and that is exactly what I did.

CHAPTER EIGHT
NATALIA

The water coming from the massage jets was doing me no justice. I had the shower head between my legs. Fucking Von was something I was trying to steer clear of, but nobody made my body feel like he did. I kept imagining the way he blessed me with that long, pretty thing that he walked around with. My mind kept going back to thoughts of him licking my kitty and how he always did it. That man was so nasty when it came to pleasing me. My hand slowly found its way to my personal treasure box.

My body burned to feel his touch, and since he wasn't there, I only could use my imagination and my memory of how he flipped and twisted my body in ways I never knew could happen. I let my fingers run down my body until they found my clit. After rubbing it for a few seconds, I replaced my fingers with the shower head. I let my fingers travel all the way down to the entrance of my kitty, then I pulled my lip into my mouth as I closed my eyes while picturing Von's face.

I placed my fingers in my mouth, moaning at the taste of my own juices. Getting my fingers wet, I slid one between my pussy lips, moving it back and forth just to tease myself. Those movements and the shower had me ready to cum, but I couldn't. It was too soon.

"Oh, baby, fuck." I moaned. Of course, in my head, it was Von's tongue there and not my finger or this showerhead.

I let my finger into my warm tunnel, curling it and doing the come here motion. "Yes. Shit!" I screamed.

If I said this wasn't the second best feeling in the world, I would be lying. It could have been first, but Von ranked number one in my book. Nothing could compare to what he did to me, which was why it was so hard to leave him alone.

My toes began to curl as I pulled and pushed my finger faster and faster. I used my other hand to move the shower head in a circular motion on my clit at the same pace.

"Fuckkkk," I moaned, dragging the K as I creamed all over my fingers.

I sat back in the tub, catching my breath.

"Damn, girl, all you had to do was call me, and I would have come and given you what your ass was just thinking about," Javon said, making me jump.

I didn't even know he was in the bathroom watching me. I could've sworn his ass was asleep. Although I was still mad at him for having bitches call his phone, kicking him out in the middle of the night was something we both agreed I wouldn't do, so as much as I wanted to, I didn't.

Looking over at him, I pondered if the dick would be worth going against what I stood for. On one hand, I was pissed, and on the other hand, I knew we wouldn't leave each other alone. My mom was always preaching to us about how it didn't make sense for us to make a big deal out of something if we wasn't going to leave the man alone in the first place. Since I was hot, high, and horny, I said, *fuck my thoughts*.

"I want you, and right now," I admitted with a smirk plastered on my face.

Javon reached the tub, and the bulge in his pants made it look like they would burst open at any second, freeing the thing that made all my right thinking leave my brain. My best friend was held hostage in them Ethikas, and I wanted him free.

Javon got on his knees and pulled me out of the water to the edge of my jacuzzi tub. He licked his lips once as he stared into my eyes. I watched as he licked my pearl really fast, then again slowly. I let my head fall as my back arched. Javon was holding my waist, and I was glad he was because I did not want to slip and fall back into the tub.

"You taste so good!" He moaned before making a slurping sound. Javon licked me around and around, driving me insane. I would always be crazy about him. I was dickmatized, and I didn't even think that was a real word.

"Oh, shit!" I moaned when he slid his tongue in and out of my hole. He was tongue fucking me so good that I grabbed the back of his head and started to grind my hips into his face. He sucked on my clit while he finger fucked me. "I could eat this shit all day," he confessed, and I would let him.

"You gon' make me cum, Von. Daddy, I am about to cum," I whimpered, trying to move away from him.

My stomach tightened, and this man wasn't letting up. I tried to push him back, but he slapped my hands away. Javon snatched me back and continued to eat. I felt like God had taken me away for a second—not a long one, just a brief second. When my next orgasm hit, my eyes were closed tight. I chewed on my bottom lip with my head tilted back. The moan I wanted to release was stuck in my throat. Tears left my eyes because he just would not stop. I wasn't even sure I wanted him to.

"Fuck, girl, you trying to drown me." He smiled, licking his lips, all while releasing that monster from his boxers.

"Daddy, come here. Let me tell you how all I can think about right now is why I'm not tasting you. My mouth is watering, and I want your dick in my mouth. Why are you not busting down my throat? Huh? I know you like that shit." I sucked my bottom lip in and lowered my gaze.

Von walked back over to me, pulled me up, and we made our way into the bedroom. As I lay back on the bed with my head hanging off the edge, I guided him to stand over me. Then, I licked from the bottom of him to the tip. I kissed my way back down and then back up, leaving no spot untouched. I let my teeth graze over the tip while my hands locked at his base. Sucking Von's dick was something I had fallen in love with. I loved doing it just as much as he loved eating my coochie. While kissing and licking the tip of his dick, I began to do the two-hand twist.

I spat on it and jerked my hands, getting him all wet. When I felt him twitch, I knew he was anticipating my next move, just like I wanted him to.

Taking some time to pay attention to his balls, I licked them slowly before pulling them into my mouth one by one and humming on them. Von taught me what he liked, and it was stored in my memory like my favorite song.

"Fuck." He groaned.

I tilted my head back some more, guiding him into my mouth. Making sure my mouth was nice and wet, I kept a steady pace. Bobbing my head up and down as best as I could since I was upside down, at the same time, I started to swirl my tongue around the tip.

"I could suck this dick all fucking day." I moaned after popping his dick out of my mouth, then quickly swallowing it.

I pulled it back out, slapped it on my lips a few times, and just like the human vacuum I was, I slurped him back in.

I got my breathing together as he thrusted into my mouth, and I let him fuck my face until it was too much spit in my mouth. Turning my body, I was able to blow spit bubbles on his dick. That man was looking down at me and smiling. He knew I was nasty, and I wouldn't change it if I could.

Von pulled me up and sat back in the chair that I had in my room. Slowly climbing off the bed, I walked the short distance to him, dripping wet. I slowly began to sit down, grabbing his dick and rubbing it on my clit. All the while, low moans fell from my lips and his. He took his time easing me down on him, causing a loud gasp to leave my mouth.

Placing his hands on my breasts, I took full control, bouncing up and down on him. Von placed one of my titties in his mouth.

"Baby, shit! Slow down 'fore I bust," he whispered, gripping my ass.

I stood, pushed his legs closed, and placed mine over his, leaving my feet off the floor. I instructed him to guide himself back into me before placing my hands on his knees. My ass was about to go on the ride of my life. I began to grind my hips in slow, circular motions before rocking back and forth, switching between the two. Once I started bouncing up and down, Von grabbed my hips and began to thrust upward, meeting me thrust for thrust.

"Yes... shittt!" I screamed, and my head fell forward. I was in heaven. This was pure bliss to me.

"You mine, right? Are you?" he asked, biting into my back.

I felt both pain and pleasure, and the pleasure was winning, which had me willing to agree to anything this man said. He could have asked me to jump off a cliff together, and my ass would have agreed. I began to cum just as I screamed,

"Yes!" With the way he was laying pipe, I was going to 'My Man' bitches to death.

Javon picked me up and turned me around, placing my knees on the chair. The chair leaned back, and I hoped like hell I didn't fall. I arched my back into the air, ready for him to enter me. If I fell, I fell. I was going to have a story to tell, though.

Von took his time sliding the tip and only the tip into me, then pulling all the way out and sliding back in. He did this a few times too many, so I pushed my ass back to get him fully inside me.

He only held my waist and let out a low chuckle.

When he slammed into me, it caused me to scream and the chair to make a cracking sound, which was not good.

"Baby, baby, wait. I think the chair broke." I moaned.

My head was back, and he held a handful of my hair. I hoped he had me tight enough just in case the chair decided to give up on us.

"You better take your dick, girl. Stop bitching! Don't run from me. Since when you start running from me?" Von grilled me while he continued to pound on me until I creamed all over him.

He followed right behind me, spilling all his seeds onto my back just as the chair went down, taking both of us with it. We hit the floor and cracked up laughing. It was all fun and games until his phone rang, fucking everything up.

"Answer it," I told him, tired of the bitch calling over and over.

Von sighed but picked up the phone.

"Yo, I'm busy," he said too quickly for my liking.

"Nah, tell the bitch what's really good." I placed my hands on my hips.

"Man, you tripping. Didn't I just fuck you real good? Eat ya pussy? Didn't I just tell you I want to be with you? Why you pressed behind this bitch? She not getting no dick, let alone me putting my mouth on her!" Von yelled at me.

"Well, what she calling for?" I asked.

"Kimmy, what you want? My bitch tripping on me 'cause you keep calling. Can you please stop? If you trying to grab, call my business phone," he said and hung up.

"She don't need to call no phone," I fussed.

"You know ain't nobody stopping my money. I fucks with you, but the moment you step between me and my money, that shit dead." He looked me in my eyes, letting me know he was serious before he walked out of the room and climbed into the shower.

I lay back on my bed, not really feeling satisfied by how things had gone. Closing my eyes, I drifted off to sleep.

CHAPTER NINE

KASH

I watched as Amarie grabbed the grapes from the fridge that she had in my office. She had been home for almost a month, and physically, she was doing a hell of a lot better. My baby had picked up weight and all. However, mentally, I could tell she was a little fucked up, and so was I.

Since the shit happened, Amarie's attitude had been on a different level, and I wasn't even sure how to move with her. One minute she was cool, and the next, she didn't want anyone around her. She was having a hard time trusting people, and I didn't know how her brain was working. She had displayed distrust with me a few times, and I never gave her reason to feel like I would do wrong by her.

Looking around, I had to laugh at myself. When we discussed merging our companies, I didn't think Amarie would take my office and add her own shit to it. In my mind, she would work from her office, and I would work from mine. Lately, I had been finding myself stressed about a lot of shit, and usually, coming to work gave me peace of mind. Now, I would leave home, come to work, and about an hour later, she would arrive with donuts and shit like everything was all good.

As much as I had grown to love Amarie, I was starting to see little things about her that I didn't like. For one, she was holding me accountable for her doing a few days in jail. The whole time, I was out there doing my best to make sure she didn't do too much time. I didn't even understand how she was mad at me. The moment they gave her bail, I paid that shit in full without a second thought. She didn't even say thank you when she saw me. This girl simply climbed into the car and went into her little shell. Yet, she hated when I brought it up because she felt like it reminded her of the time she did, and nobody knew what she went through.

"Baby, do you want to order lunch for later?" she asked.

"Nah, I'm good. If you want to, you can. I'm going to swing by a few of the houses and collect rent. I'm also going over to the other building to see how things are coming along over there."

"What's the problem? I feel like you don't want me here. I will go over to the other building if it's a problem. I made you breakfast, and you didn't eat it. You had to quickly get here, and now I'm trying to do lunch with you, and you're skipping out on that as well," she snapped, rolling her neck.

"Relax. My baby don't need you getting worked up. I am just trying to handle shit. Your ass is bipolar or something. One minute you want to be left alone, and the next, you want me to kiss your ass. We grown. Communication works both ways."

There I was, telling her how communication worked, yet I wasn't really trying to communicate either. I really just wanted to get away from her for a while before I snapped on her. Amarie was so used to me just letting her get her way that she didn't even know it was another side to me.

"What do you mean 'relax,' Kasha? We are at work, not at

home, so I'm going to chill, but best believe we will revisit this conversation at home," she sternly stated.

She could say whatever she wanted because my ass was not going to be there. I was going out for drinks with the guys, and it was much needed. Amarie and I clearly needed some time apart because I was liable to say some mean shit to her that she needed to hear. I was going to tell her anyway, but with me being fed up with her, it would be delivered wrong, and I didn't need that.

Getting back to work, I looked at the numbers for the month and was happy with them. One of my Airbnbs in Florida was rented for an entire month. Being the nice person that I was, I gave the family of five a nice discount for their stay. My Airbnb out in Atlanta was also rented, but that one was only for five days. I had already made twice the amount I had spent on Amarie's bail. Money was flowing in, and business was going great. However, my personal life was horrible. I hadn't had my dick sucked in a week or two, and getting pussy was like picking a hang nail. Just thinking about it made me mad.

Standing up, I closed my computer down and walked out of the office. Before I left, I made my rounds, checking to ensure everybody was good.

I drove to the properties that I was rehabbing, and the apartments were coming along great. I did not expect them to be ready for another year. I had bought those abandoned homes on Chester Avenue, where a bunch of college kids and other people lived. Just off the area, the apartments ran around nine to twelve hundred dollars a month. Each house was about four stories and held three to four apartments. Mine were going to be more spacious. I had four houses, and I was making them each two apartments.

I would see the money from it until my kid was ten, and on

his or her tenth birthday, I would gift the houses to the child. I wanted a daughter so bad because I wanted to teach her to be a boss ass young lady. Plus, I heard girls were more attached to their dads, and what would be better than to have a daddy's girl? Yet, if I had a son, I would do my best to steer him clear of the streets, but with an uncle like Von, who I knew would think this was his child as well because he already did, shit would be hard. My son would see life from both angles and if he were in the streets and moved like Von, I wouldn't be too upset.

"Hey, Kasha, my guys are just finishing up. We have to wait for the city to come out and the inspections to get done before we move on to the next phase." My contractor showed me around the building.

The outside was brick and looked good. The windows were covered in some blue shit, I guess for installation purposes. I did not ask too many questions because Tony and his crew had been working with my dad and me for years, and we never had any problems.

"Okay. I will make that call now. Did you need anything else from me? How is the layout looking?" I made conversation with him.

"Good, good. I say, give or take a few months, and things will be almost ready to go. I still believe you should put a laundry room in the basement for the units. There's enough space, man, and we can make a separate entrance. We still got time before the walls are put up. We can have the electrical team run the wires and things through." Tony had been in America for a while, yet his English still wasn't too good.

"If you think you can do it, do it. Just send me the bill," I said as I typed on my phone.

My mom's friend was an inspector, and I had her private and business number. People loved to steal pipes and shit, so I was texting her private phone to get her out as quickly as I could. If I took too long and gave the smokers an opportunity, that would cause me a great setback, and I'd lose some money. I wasn't trying to go through that. I sat on top of my car and watched as Tony and his guys cleaned up their mess while I smoked. I was smoking way more than I usually did, and that was crazy to me.

Amarie called my phone, and instead of declining the call like I wanted to, I picked up.

"Did you forget about the appointment today? It is in an hour if you want to meet me there. Von just pulled up. He's getting on my nerves. I don't even know why you would tell him," she snapped as I heard Von in the background, yelling about finding out the gender of the baby.

Of course, I asked him to be the child's god dad, and he wanted to do all the shit that my mom and them had done when my sister was younger. It was a whole ceremony, and her godparents gave her a middle name.

"I'm going to meet you there. I'm like fifteen minutes away from there anyway, so let me know when you pulling up." I hung the phone up and climbed in my car, thanking God I decided to smoke outside. I would have to look in my trunk for a different shirt.

My phone buzzed again, and I looked down at it.

"Don't forget you have that business dinner tonight with that other company you were trying to invest in. Your suit came yesterday. You also need to try it on," she reminded me like she was my assistant, who, by the way, didn't remind me about this shit when I was just there.

"Cool," I dryly replied and hung up the phone.

Tony walked over to a car, and a girl stepped out, looking good as hell. I knew she was some sort of Spanish, but I didn't really know what. Her hair hung down her back, and she had a fat ass that I could tell was bought just by her legs. Climbing in my car, I pulled off and slowly drove to the hospital. Once I found parking, I searched my trunk for another shirt and then swapped out, making sure to spray a little cologne on it just so I wouldn't smell like weed.

Amarie pulled up a few minutes later, and we walked into the building together with Von right behind us.

"We really about to have a son, sis," he joked because he knew how much I wanted a girl.

"I know my son gon' be handsome. He gon' look just like his mommy." Amarie beamed.

I could not lie; my girl was beautiful. Her hair, which she had been wearing out lately, was curled, falling a little past her shoulders. She had on a pair of dress pants and a white blouse that showed off her little baby bump, and the pair of Jimmy Choo heels gave her a little height.

I went over to the desk and checked her in while she sat down as Von went to the snack machine. Today was just an ultrasound, and I was happy because sometimes the other appointments were long as hell for no reason.

"Here, everything you asked for." He dropped the snacks on Amarie, and I wanted to knock his ass out and hers.

Amarie quickly opened the hot fries and popped two in her mouth. Von had the nerve to be eating a cake and chips as well.

"You out of pocket for that shit, bro," I whispered, and he just shrugged.

"Our son wanted some chips, so I got them." He laughed.

"Say my godson or some shit. You keep saying 'our son' like we having a baby together, and she just carrying it," I replied to him and his madness.

"How ever you look at it, that's both our son," he insisted, and Amarie laughed.

Deciding to just shut up because he wouldn't stop saying

it, I looked through my phone. I had recently made a new Instagram, and I already had over ten thousand followers, but I did not know how. I scrolled through people's stories, not really watching most of them.

"Amarie," I heard.

We all stood and walked to the back.

"Hey, I'm Julia, and I will be doing your ultrasound today. Are we finding out what baby is or no?" she asked as she walked to a room.

"Yes. Well, you can put it in an envelope and give it to God-dad," Amarie told her.

"Okay, cool beans. I need you to take off this shirt and put on a gown. So, God-dad, would you mind stepping out?" The lady looked at Von, who almost ran out of the room at the mention of Amarie having to take her shirt off.

Once he was out of the room, Amarie changed into the gown and lay back on the chair. The lady fixed everything how she needed it to be, and then I got Von. We watched the screen while she talked us through each thing she did. Seconds later, my baby's big ole head popped up on the screen.

"So, you will sporadically see some blue and red on the screen. I'll be measuring the baby's blood flow, length, heart-beat, and everything else. I will be sure to stop and answer any questions you have," she told us before she got to work.

The pictures were in 3D, and I could already see that the baby would have full lips like me. My eyes were stuck to the screen as I watched my child move around. I could not believe that I had gone half on creating a whole person. Hearing snif-fles, I looked up at Amarie, who had silent tears falling from her eyes. My eyes then traveled to Javon, and I couldn't believe this nigga.

"Shut up," he said, quickly using the back of his hands to wipe his eyes.

I let out a small laugh. This muthafucka was crazy.

"Alright. I'm going to turn the screen. God-dad, would you mind turning off that screen up there that Mommy can see. I'm going to see what baby is."

Von did exactly what she said, and I tried hard as hell to read his facial expression, but there wasn't one besides the look of amazement.

"Alright, so you see it?" she asked, and he nodded.

"Okay, we are all done. I'm going to print pictures and remove the gender photo." The lady wiped off Amarie's stomach and left the room.

"Man, y'all got a family. One day, I'm gon' have one, and y'all gon' be the god parents as well. What y'all doing is amazing. Y'all really a power couple and our child deserves you two as its parents." Von dapped me up.

I was going to be the best father in the world. I would do everything I could to make sure my child felt the same love from me as I felt from my parents, and that was a promise.

CHAPTER TEN

NATALIA

I walked into my house and had to laugh. Javon was sitting in my living room with a big cheese steak that was damn near gone. He had his feet kicked up on my table and his game connected to my living room TV. How he got inside my house was beyond me.

"You was out all night? I'm confused because you know you got a man at home." He glanced at me before his eyes went back to the game.

"What you mean? First of all, you're my man one day and not the next day. Besides, I was not out all night. It is three in the morning. How you even get in here?" I questioned.

I was feeling the effects of the drinks, and I was tired. But I was more tired of him and going back and forth. If anything, I felt like he owed it to me and more to himself to figure out what he was doing because as quickly as we got our shit together was a quickly as he was back in the clubs with bitches on his lap. Now, I didn't mind him getting dances from strippers or even being in the strip club. At the end of the day, he was a man, and I loved that place just as much as he did.

However, he shouldn't have been taking them bitches home or any other bitch, for that matter. Javon thought with his little head and not his big head when it came to females.

"Either way, my wife ain't gon' be coming in at no three in the morning." He spoke to me like I cared.

"Well, good thing I ain't your wife." Sliding my shoes off my feet, I walked up the stairs and into my bathroom, stripping myself of my clothes.

After starting the water in the shower, I waited for it to heat up before climbing in. As soon as the water hit my body, I relaxed. Feeling a cool breeze, I looked behind me and saw Javon stepping in. That thing between his legs was so long and pretty that it made my mouth water. Grabbing my rag, I quickly washed my body and tried to step out of the shower but was pulled back.

"Man, stop playing with me. Look at my dick. He hard as shit, waiting on you. How you gon' let daddy be horny like that? Come on, ma," he practically begged.

"Javon, I'm not playing with you. You think you supposed to come in here, sling dick, and keep me to yourself while I share you," I replied.

He spat this girlfriend shit all the time but was still talking to bitches.

"You still tripping off bitches calling my phone? I'm not fucking them. I'm not giving them bitches no bread or nothing."

"But you giving them bitches conversation, and you allowing them bitches to smile in your face," I snapped as I got out of the shower, and he did not stop me.

"Insecure ass bitch," I heard him say.

I wanted to act like Yvette from *Baby Boy* and do the screaming and flipping out. Instead, I kept walking. There was nothing insecure about me. I knew that if a person came into my world and caught the vibe I had, they wouldn't want to leave, which was why I didn't get why Javon did the shit he did. One minute, we were good, and the next, he was back on his hoe shit. It seemed to just be in him to be that way.

After drying my body, I slipped into a nightshirt and climbed into my bed. I could not lie like Von being in my bed every night didn't feel good to me. However, I would survive if he wasn't.

———

Tonight, we were supposed to be celebrating my mom's fiftieth birthday, but my mind was everywhere else. I had to pull up because everything was already paid for, and we couldn't switch the dates. My mom and all her friends were having fun, but I just couldn't. It did not feel right without my two sisters in the building partying with me. Amarie was there, but she was ducked off. She and my mom had talked, and she wasn't really feeling where my mom was coming from, which was understandable on both parts.

Mentally, I was not there, and I damn sure was in no mood to party. All I could think about was how this shit happened and how it spiraled out of control so quickly. I was trying my hardest to produce different solutions, but each one I came up with was out of my control. The only thing that kept playing in my mind was for me to somehow get Nakari to admit that she was lying on Amarie. If I could get that and record it, I could get Amarie off.

"Why we can't stop beefing and just settle down?" Von whispered in my ear.

"Because you just can't stop messing with bitches," I replied.

"How is Nakari holding up? Even though the bitch got my

daughter's mom in a messed up situation," he said before looking around him.

Javon was the only one who knew what Amarie was having. He had just let it slip, and now I would have to keep it a secret too. Their main concern was having a healthy baby, no matter their gender.

"I don't know. She been talking to my mom more than me, and my mom really ain't saying much 'cause she knows how we all feel about everything." I sat there with my leg bouncing up and down, on the verge of tears.

"Look, you got to relax and learn how to enjoy the moment. Shit happens. It'll figure itself out." Von spoke to me.

He walked off and grabbed a bottle, taking a shot with my mom, who was having so much fun. I looked over at Amarie, who was smiling at everyone having fun. Saying fuck it, I grabbed a bottle from behind the bar, cracked it open, and took a long sip. I needed to feel the Casamigos going down. After a few more sips, I felt a little hot and wanted to dance. Standing up, I started to move around the dance floor like it was my birthday. I danced my way over to my mom, and she smiled.

"I'm glad to see you up out of that funk," she tried to whisper but failed.

Uncle Luke was blasting, and the way my mama and her friends were cutting up, I made a mental note to ask her if she would be on that Freak Nik documentary. My mom was bent over, shaking her ass, while her friend was next to her, humping the air. These old bitches were wild.

"My girl is throwing that thing." Amarie laughed, standing next to me.

I swore this was how we were going to act when we got old. Kash parents were even there, and my mom was trying to teach his mom how to "pop that pussy," as she called it. They were drinking Mad Dog 2020, Old E, and Belvedere while smoking weed, so I knew it was bound to be a long night.

"Ain't she? How you holding up?" I asked, rubbing her belly.

"I'm taking this shit day by day. Hell, I'd rather be in jail than in that house with my man, who is upset with me, and I know it's my fault," she admitted.

"Get it together. You have a funny way of being angry at everyone when somebody does something to you. Kash is a good man. Don't lose him because you gon' regret it," I replied.

"You right. I love you, cousin, and I'm sorry if I ever made you feel some type of way. I do not want you to feel like you have to choose either. I'm your cousin, but Nakari is your little sister, and it's not your fault she did what she did."

That lifted a weight off my shoulders.

"Y'all are both my little sisters, and I love you too. I'm about to head home. I'm tired, and my classes start back up in the morning," I told her. I was going to school to become a kindergarten teacher.

I did my rounds of goodbyes and noticed Javon was not there. When I walked outside into the parking lot, I looked around for his car, which wasn't out there either. Instantly, I felt like he was up to no good if he didn't even come to say goodbye. I pulled out of the parking lot and drove by his block since it was only a few minutes away. I circled the block a few times before I parked a few cars down to watch the new trap houses he had set up. His car was parked, but the windows were so tinted that he could have been in there watching me, just like I was looking for him, and I would have never known.

Boom!

My car rocked. Looking over, I cursed myself for parking on the corner. Immediately, I opened my car door and jumped out to look at the damage. My car was fucked up, but the damage to my heart was worse. Von had stepped out of the driver seat of the car that had crashed into mine and was cursing while Kimmy stepped out of the passenger seat. I knew it was her from the pictures she had sent to his phone when I went through their messages.

"Damn, baby, the head was so good, you done fucked this bitch car up." Kimmy laughed like shit was funny.

Von was standing there, staring at me like he knew he fucked up, which he did. I could tell by his stance that his dumb ass was drunk, which gave me the upper hand. I quickly snatched Kimmy by her long ass braids, bringing her close to me. I started to pound my fist repeatedly into the back of her head. She was swinging wildly, but I was already too hurt for her little hits to faze me. I slung her against my car and tried to put her head through the window.

I didn't forget about all the shit talking she did over the phone. She may have been right about Javon not leaving her alone, but she was wrong about her beating my ass. I took her head and rammed it into the side of the car again before I slung her to the ground. She was holding my hair tightly, so I almost went down with her, but I didn't. Even in heels, I managed to stay on my feet. While she was on the ground, I dragged her ass.

"That's enough. Come on, 'fore the cops come, and you make shit hot. She not even fighting back. Just screaming for help." Javon pulled at my hands.

That only made me madder. Not only did he leave me to be with the bitch, but now he was protecting her from an ass whooping.

"Aye, Clips! Help me, man," Javon called to one of his workers.

I was not letting up on her. I wanted her to think twice

about telling me how she would beat my ass and drag me all through the streets.

"Ain't you said you was gon' drag me, bitch?" I yanked her harder.

Von had lifted me off the ground and was trying to turn me away from her, but I kept a hold on her ass, punching her anywhere my hands would land.

"Come on, Natalia. Please let her go. I fucked up and let her suck my dick. I'm sorry," he said.

"If I let this bitch go, you gon' get off me? I want to get the fuck away from you. I hate you so bad, Javon!" I cried.

He placed me on my feet, so I let her go and darted up the stairs to his trap house. If I was smart and thinking, I would have gone in his pockets and taken his keys, so I could leave.

"Damn, you did a number on that bitch," Earl said.

"She said she was gon' beat my ass when she saw me. All I did was show her that shit wasn't true. Can one of y'all take me home?" I asked while Von and the bitch stood outside, having a screaming match.

"Go home, dumb ass bitch. You sucked my dick, and that's it. That's all you ever do," he yelled before walking toward me.

"Close the door and lock it," I told Earl, and he looked at me like I was dumb.

"You want to show your ass, huh?" Javon walked up to me.

"Boy, fuck you. Can you give me your car, so I can leave?" I snapped.

"Nah, you pulled up here for what? Huh? To talk? What's up?" he said.

"Okay, watch this."

Pulling my phone out, I sent my friend a text. He lived around the corner, and I knew he would take me home. I would have gotten an Uber, but I didn't have an account.

Javon looked at me and laughed before he walked outside and waited on the porch. I sat there for about ten minutes until my ride texted me that he was outside. Walking out of the house, I went down the steps but was quickly snatched back by my hair.

"Bitch, you crazy? You want me to turn the fuck up, don't you? I ain't ever played with you like that," Von spat.

"You just played with me. You forgot? You know what the fuck this is, nigga. You play, I play too. Plus, you know how I suck dick, so I hope that shit was worth it, 'cause you know how nasty I give it up," I taunted him.

"Stop playing, and come on, girl. Got me out my damn bed," Dee yelled from the car before he rolled the window back up.

Von pushed past me and used the butt of his gun to break Dee's window, so he could pull the car door open.

"You know this bitch sucks dick for buffalo wing platters, huh?" Von dumb ass yelled as he snatched Dee's punk ass out of the car.

"Javon, stop. You better not hit him. He don't even like girls!" I screamed and grabbed Javon's arm as he brought it down, ready to pistol whip Dee.

Dee's ass was screaming, and I wanted to laugh so bad. He was in a black silk pajama set. That man liked the same thing I did, which was why I called him. He didn't wear wigs and all that, but he was very feminine.

"Man, what the fuck?" Von dropped him on the ground.

"Oh, thank you, Lord." Dee scrambled back into the car and was about to leave my ass.

I ran over to the passenger side and jumped in.

"How the fuck was I about to get home?" I asked him.

"Bitch, I don't know, but that strong, fine ass man was about to send me home, and I ain't talking about to 2617. He was about to send me to the upper room. And why are you sucking dick for buffalo wing platters?" he asked, causing me to double over in laughter.

"It's not like that, but it is like that. Bitch, I was hungry one day, and his ass had some shit to do. I ain't want to go out since I was cleaning the house, and you know a bitch was cleaning cleaning. I asked him to get me some, and he said, 'suck my dick,' so I did. You know I love sucking his dick. I told you that," I said.

"Bitch, did you get a buffalo wing platter?" he asked.

"Did I? Bitch, you know he sent me twenty wings, a pizza, and a soda," I joked.

We cracked jokes the rest of the ride. Every time Dee drove fast and the wind blew into the car, he reminded me that I was paying for him to get a new window. I didn't mind because he pulled up when I needed him, even though he almost lost his life.

CHAPTER ELEVEN

NAKARI

"You know you ain't shit. That girl never did nothing wrong to you. Don't you think she been through enough? I was already making it worse, and you went ahead and did the most hurtful thing, though. She's having a baby, and you could make her lose it. You selfish. You was dealing with your own demons, and you placed it on somebody else."

DeJuan sat in the corner of my cell. He was chilling hard on the floor. His legs were stretched out, and he was in the same clothes he had on when he died. I could even smell the strong scent of fire. However, the smell of the crack that I wanted so badly was even stronger.

"You know I never took you for the bitch you turned out to be. My mom was right when she said a female would be my downfall, but I never knew it would be you. From the day I met you, I knew you wasn't shit, just like me, which was why I preyed on you. I wanted to hurt Amarie, but not like this. You a crackhead, now. Your family is going to hate you. You should have stayed inside that room with me and burnt to death. It would have been a hell of a lot easier for you than this. You not built for jail," he taunted me as he got closer.

DeJuan pulled a piece of crack from his pocket and inched closer to me. The smell of shit radiated off him, but I didn't care. I reached my hand out for the crack, then he pulled back and slapped the shit out of me. The slap was nothing to me. I wanted the drug more. He slapped me again. This time, harder.

Jumping up, I locked eyes with my cell mate. My ass was dreaming about smoking crack, and that was crazy. Yet, the shit smell was not from the dream. LaLa was about five foot nine and was damn near three hundred and something pounds. She was really pretty in the face but was built like a linebacker. I wasn't sure if she wasn't wiping her ass all the way or what, but she always smelled like shit.

"Why my breakfast not fixed, bitch?" she asked me, and I looked at her like she was crazy.

"Who the fuck you talking to? I ain't your bitch, and breakfast was already served. You must have missed it, playing in somebody's ass because that's what your hands smell like. And I know for damn sure you ain't slap me!" I barked.

"Yeah, I did. You were in here tossing and turning and reaching out for something. I called your name, and you ain't answer. It's time for showers. I know you don't like missing them." She smirked.

"You should have took one first." I stood, and she pushed me.

Grabbing the radio from my bed, I swung it, hitting her in the head. This bitch didn't even seem fazed, so I started swinging on her. LaLa started punching me back, and I swear, each blow she delivered to my head felt like I was being hit with a baseball bat. Seconds later, her friends were inside the cell, and they were all snatching me off the bed. I fought back for as long as I could before I found myself balled up on the floor, being stomped.

"That's enough. I think the bitch got it," Ramona called out.

She was the leader in their group, and I was sure her ass got a good couple of punches off on me too. She looked at me and nodded for me to walk with her. Once I pulled myself off the ground, we headed toward the showers, and I was scared as hell.

"You can't be fucking with LaLa. She is protected in here, mami," she let me know.

"Tell her to leave me alone then, or y'all gon' have to jump me every time. I'm not her bitch, and she needs to keep her shitty fingers to herself."

"I'll talk to her. There's something else we need to talk about, though," she said as we made it to a part of the showers where no guards were.

Ramona began to take off her clothes, and she nodded for me to do so as well. I was hesitant at first, but when she flashed a small baggie of the white substance I had grown to love, my ass moved a little quicker. She placed some on her finger and snorted it before she gave me some. I sniffed the substance off her finger and rested my head back, enjoying the feel of the drug running through my body. We stepped under the water, and Ramona made a head gesture. Two of her girls appeared, and the guard who was standing near the showers turned her head.

Ramona pulled me close to her and pecked my lips a few times before she slowly slid her tongue into my mouth while keeping her eyes locked on mine. I let myself get lost in the kiss as the drug really kicked in. I was floating on cloud nine while our tongues wrestled for dominance before I let her win. I moaned into her mouth then let my hands go up and rub her breasts.

Ramona grabbed me by the front of my neck and applied a little pressure, causing my pussy to leak. She kissed me all over my face before letting her lips travel down my body. Ramona kissed and sucked on my neck for a second, then moved down to my boobs. I watched her as she twirled her tongue around one of my nipples while lightly pinching the other.

"Do I make you feel good?" Ramona asked.

Quickly nodding my head, I let my moans give her the answer she was looking for. I did my best to keep them low, but it was hard.

Ramona switched her mouth to my other nipple before letting her tongue travel down my stomach. It dipped into my belly button, then met the most sensitive spot on my body. My leg was now draped over her shoulder, and my back was against the wall.

Ramona flicked her tongue across my clit, making my toes curl and my body shiver. I swore she might have been spelling her name or whatever she was doing with the different tricks she did with her tongue. Ramona slid two fingers inside me while she sucked my clit into her mouth and then let her tongue slide back and forth across it. My back arched up bizarre the moment she inserted another finger into me. At the same time, her mouth still worked on my clit.

My body began to shake, and Ramona pumped her finger faster. She was making my stay in jail well worth it, and I was sure I would not mind being her bitch if it came with a get high and head like this. This girl never unlatched from my pearl while swirling her tongue in slow circles.

I screamed out in pleasure, letting her lick up all the juices that spilled from me.

Ramona stopped and wiped her mouth. She then stood to

her feet, leaving me doubled over, trying to catch my breath. My body was quickly slammed against the wall, and a blade was placed on my neck.

"The pussy tasted good, never tasted better, but I was paid to give you a message. You better figure out how to change that statement, and quickly, or the next time, I'm going to have you in here looking like you couldn't take life no more and decided to end it."

Ramona had me scared to move. The high that I once felt was gone, and I felt the piss running down my leg.

"Okay!" I cried, scared for my life.

"Good. Make sure y'all take care of her." Ramona placed some more powder under my nose, and I sniffed it all.

The girls she had waiting by the door walked over to me with a small tool that looked like a plastic covered flashlight. One girl dropped to her knees and began to feast on my kitty. She moaned my name and got nothing in response, while the other girl placed more drugs underneath my nose. I sniffed it until it was all gone. She even stuck her finger in my mouth, letting me suck the rest off.

One of the girls reached over me and smacked the other girl's ass. The one between my legs used her tool thing and slid it inside me while the other girl let her tongue travel up my ass. She licked around my asshole in slow circles. The entire time, I kept my hands in the hair of the girl in front of me. She was using whatever the tool was to fuck me, and it felt so good. She was going at a steady pace, making sure to hit my spot every time.

Somehow, we ended up on the floor. I was bent over with my ass in the air. The girl had one side of the tool in her and the other side in me. The other girl was on her back, and my face was buried deep in her pussy.

She wined her pussy into my face, and I let my tongue into her wet cave as she moved at her own pace.

"Ohh, fuck. Baby, this a good one. Ramona just made this special." She moaned.

"Time is up," the guard yelled, and we all hopped up.

I grabbed the towel that was left behind and wrapped myself up.

On my way out, Ramona winked at me.

"You better not forget what you are supposed to do, or your time here will end. Make it quick," the girl whispered in my ear, reminding me that them bitches were just about to kill me.

I walked back to my cell and sat on the bed with a smile on my face. My pussy was tingling, and it felt so good. As I lay back on the bed, my heart felt like it was racing too fast for my liking. I grabbed my chest and held it, waiting for the rapid beat to slow down. I felt like my shit was going to jump out of my chest. My head was also pounding, and I needed some sort of help. It was hard for me to get up, but I tried to pull myself up.

"You not about to go nowhere." LaLa pushed me back down on the bed.

"Please, I need help. I don't know what they gave me!" I cried.

I was sweating, and I felt like I was about to die. Each time I looked over, DeJuan was sitting there in the same spot as earlier.

"Leave me alone. Please go away!" I screamed at him, but all he did was laugh.

Each time I tried to get up, LaLa pushed me back down. DeJuan was now walking closer to me, and I wanted him to get away.

"Why you kill him?" LaLa asked.

"I didn't mean to. It was an accident. Now he will not leave me alone. I think I'm going crazy!" I screamed.

My heart was beating so fast that it hurt.

DeJuan placed his hand over my mouth, and I felt like I couldn't breathe. My body began to shake, and it felt like I was choking on something.

"Don't ever think you gon' have one up on me, bitch. Not when my man and my brother got pull. I hope you rot in hell." Amarie laughed in my ear.

LaLa was holding a cellphone up to my ear that she had pulled from somewhere.

The call disconnected, and she tucked it away before running out and screaming.

"Yo, she needs help. It looks like she took something and is having a bad reaction to it," LaLa performed.

I tried to talk, but I still couldn't breathe. My eyes slowly closed, yet I was still trying to let them know who did this to me. I did not deserve this. I gave up trying to fight the feeling and let the darkness welcome me. Everyone would think I overdosed. My story would never be told, and nobody would ever care. It always happened this way with me, especially when it came to my cousin, who came in and tried to take away everything that belonged to me.

I was jealous at heart, and for no reason. Now, there I was, looking like a junkie, when Amarie was really the cause of my demise.

CHAPTER TWELVE
AMARIE

We were all sitting inside the hospital crying. I was crying because I knew I was about to be free, and because shit had to come to this. Nakari was my cousin, and I felt somewhat bad for her death, yet I knew she would always end up being a problem for me. I sat on the chair with my leg bouncing up and down while my auntie acted an ass. I hated that I was the cause of this pain they had to go through, and the sad thing was, this was something I would take to the grave.

"Auntie, come on. Get up," I said as my voice cracked.

It pained me really bad to see her hurting, but I would do it all again if I had to.

Having my cousin killed was not something I was proud of. It was not even something I would have thought to do, but when Von mentioned it, I couldn't help wanting to act on it. We had LaLa record Nakari saying it was an accident, then LaLa acted like she was Nakari and wrote a sad little message to go with it about how it was haunting her, and she had to come clean because she was going crazy in there. Once she sent it, she cleared the phone, wiped away any prints, and placed it in Nakari's things, which would clear my name.

"That was my baby. Why she turn to drugs? I wish she would have told me what was bothering her." My auntie had yet another meltdown.

We were waiting for her to go back and view the body to identify her, even though they knew it was her. My auntie was scared while Natalia was quiet. She was crying but not aloud. She was always able to hide her emotions.

"Look, Ma, we have to pull it together for her. You know Nakari didn't want to be put in the ground, so if you want to do something small for the family and then have her cremated, we can," Natalia said as she pulled her mother off the floor.

The police took them both to the back, and hearing my aunt's screams sent chills through my body. I wanted to be there for them in ways that I could not be. I did not know how to fake it like what happened wasn't my fault when it was. I sat there, battling my emotions, before I got up and walked out.

"Oh, God! What did I do?" I cried as I slid down the wall.

I had fucked up and caused my family some trauma that I should have never done. My conscience was eating at me, and I wanted to tell them what I did, but they would hate me, and I couldn't have that. There I was, happy to erase a problem, but only causing a bigger one.

"You can't let that shit eat you up. You had to do what was best for you. She would have done that shit to you," Von told me, and I laughed.

"That's what's crazy. Even though I know I made the right choice, I still feel like I was wrong. That is not me. I'm not a killer," I expressed.

"And you still not," he told me.

"But I made the call."

"Did you? She did them drugs on her own and would have

done it regardless, so she killed herself, and we gon' leave it like that. You wasn't there to make her sniff that shit. We all know she did it willingly."

"Thanks for that, bro," I said and stood up.

"Anytime. Keep my god child safe and stop that crying shit. When it's you or somebody else in any situation, you better choose you and do whatever you got to do to come out on top." He stood and walked away from me.

———

Two days later, I sat in the backseat of the limo with my aunt and cousin as we drove through the hood. My father was with us, but like always, he was quiet. I looked out the window as we drove through our old hood. My aunt wasted no time and spared no expense for Nakari. She just kept saying how she did not want her daughter laid up in that place for too long, and how everything that was going on was her fault. My auntie did not realize that she did a great job raising us. We made dumb decisions on our own because we thought it was cool and fun.

My aunt had Nakari's casket open, and she looked so beautiful. Of course, her skin was darker, and she looked smaller due to her drug use, but she still looked beautiful. Her hair was in a thirty-inch bust down with a middle part that was her favorite hairstyle. She was dressed in Dior from head to toe, and her makeup was beautifully done. She looked like she was asleep. I had spoken my peace to her in a low whisper when we walked up to view her body.

"At least her ass don't have to stress about Capri no more. They together now." Natalia broke the silence in the limo.

"You could have waited to say that." My dad looked over at my aunt, who was just staring out the window.

I honestly felt like she was taking it so hard because she

had always been more of a friend to us than a parent. There were a lot of things we told her in confidence, and then there were things we kept to ourselves, knowing she could not hold water. We all figured that out when Natalia's boyfriend got her pregnant, and my aunt took her to get an abortion. She lectured us for weeks with her friends about how we were fucking and not being careful. By the time she was done, everyone knew what she had promised not to expose. We learned at that point to only tell her what was necessary.

Nakari had always been the one my aunt said we would have to watch. She always had jealous traits, but as we got older and closer, they didn't show anymore.

"Come on, we going inside the house. They are going to take her back to the funeral home and will call when her ashes are ready to be picked up." Natalia shook my leg, breaking me from my thinking.

I hadn't even noticed we were in front of my aunt's house. Everyone got out of their cars and made their way inside the house. My aunt had tables set up with food. She also had a little bar in the corner that somebody was controlling. Everyone had insurance, and I was sure that was what paid for all this shit. It was eighty degrees outside, and my auntie had a damn mink draped over her shoulders. I just knew her ass was sweating underneath all the black she had on.

The DJ was set up outside, and the way people filled the street, you would have thought we were having a block party. Everyone came to show Nakari love, and that made me smile.

"Aye, I just wanted to say that Nakari is with you, baby sis. I know I don't say much, and I know my niece wasn't perfect, but who was? We all have our own demons, and hers were just ones she couldn't fight. We all know the battle she faced was a hard one. Nakari was not just a girl facing demons, though. She was loving, fun, and crazy. Sis, in a time like this, I cannot imagine what you're feeling, but I do know that Nakari wouldn't want you to be down. She wouldn't want any of us to be. That girl is probably in heaven right now, turning up. So, let's turn this shit up for her. I want everyone who's driving to not get too fucked up, but if you ain't, I want you to remember this day as a good one, not a sad one. I want y'all to describe this day as a day you had a time." My dad raised his cup in the air.

I looked around and saw people raising their cups, bottles, and whatever else they had in their hands.

"To Nakari. We love you, baby. And thank you, Aaron," my auntie called out.

Everyone took a sip of their drinks, and that was all it took for the party to get started. I swore they were taking shots every three minutes. Growing tired and needing a nap, I went into the house and climbed the steps to our old bedroom. The set of bunk beds was still in there along with Natalia's single bed. Everything was still how we left it. I closed the door and turned the air conditioner on.

Climbing into my old bed, I lay underneath the covers. I felt like sleep was the only thing that helped me ease my mind and didn't have me thinking about all the bullshit that was going on.

"I'm so sorry, cousin. I swore we would never reach this point. I'm trying to forgive myself, and I forgive you. I hope you forgive me too," I said, like she would respond to me.

I felt a little breeze and took that as a sign from Nakari. Closing my eyes, I let my body relax and drifted into a deep, much needed slumber.

"I miss us all sleeping in here," Natalia said, waking me from my sleep.

I knew I wasn't asleep for that long because I would have been angry if I had gotten into a good sleep, and she woke me up. I could admit I missed it too. We would sneak in and out the window using a sheet as our ladder while my auntie was in her room getting fucked on or passed out from a long night of drinking. We would always get put on punishment when we got caught sneaking out, but we didn't care because we would all be in the room together, playing hand games and whatever else we found ourselves doing.

The pink lips phone that we had as kids still sat in the room on the nightstand. We had dialed the party line so many times on that phone, all acting older than we were. My fake name was Keisha, and I was about five to six years older than my real age. When my aunt found out we were on the party line and had actually snuck out to meet one of the guys Natalia was talking to, she damn near killed us. She beat us so bad with her yellow bat that we all missed school the next day.

"Remember that time we snuck that liquor, and Nakari's ass fell back out the window when we were sneaking in?" I laughed at the memory.

We were in our little gaucho pants from Limited Too with our cute little back out shirts that we weren't supposed to have. There was a dollar party happening, and since we had gotten in trouble at school, we couldn't go. Our asses snuck out anyway, but before we did, we stole some of my aunt' sloe gin, thinking if we didn't take that much, we would be okay. That was one of the dumbest decisions we could have made. We all had a cup a piece with orange juice like we'd seen her do so many times. By the time we made it back, we were all stumbling.

I climbed in first, and then it was Nakari's turn. Natalia was pushing her up while I was trying to pull her. This girl let go and fell. I was surprised she didn't break anything with the way she hit the ground. Her wrist was swollen but moving. Before we could get her up, my auntie ran out the door worried, and somehow, we still got a beating. We were on punishment for the entire summer.

"Yes. I ain't touched no sloe gin since. That shit was nasty but had us fucked up. This Nakari shit got me looking at life differently. I want better for myself, and I want to do better. I am learning from her mistakes and my own. We made promises to each other. I hope you remember them," Natalia said.

I nodded because I would never forget. We always said if one of us died, the other two would have to complete their bucket list and complete the person's list who died. I was glad Nakari had tried all the crazy shit already because some of the stuff, I just was not trying to do. I loved my cousin dearly, but she was a wild child, and some of that shit went against everything I stood for as a woman.

CHAPTER THIRTEEN

KASH

I sat in my office, talking on the phone to Mr. Wang. He had canceled plans with me too many times and now was requesting a meeting. Even after I told him he couldn't come to my office, he still said that he would be on his way. He kept telling me how he could change my mind if he could just talk to me in person. I was glad I had dressed in a suit today because he wouldn't take no for an answer, as if he were the one investing in my company. He had a growing photography company and event planning business. I knew that if I put money into it and helped him get clientele, I could make some extra money off him. He was good at what he did; he just did not have the funds to get everything he needed to make his business do better.

His parents also owned a hair store that was about to go out of business. I could have easily just bought it, but I didn't want to do the footwork, nor did I want to have to find people to run it. Running my own company was enough for me. I wasn't trying to do shit else but collect money and grow my family.

A few minutes later, Amarie walked into the office with Wang behind her. My baby was growing, and I could tell because Amarie's belly seemed to have grown overnight. Her once small, round belly now looked like a little basketball was in her shirt.

Amarie looked good in her little pantsuit. She had her blazer jacket unbuttoned, and her cleavage showed just a little at the top.

"Kasha, Mr. Wang was causing havoc about meeting with you. I have potential buyers waiting for you in the lobby. I'm going to take them into your other office and have them start the paperwork. I also have to run over to the other building. I have a meeting there with the lady in about an hour or so. If need be, I could have her come here," Amarie said as she grabbed paperwork off my desk. Her heels clicked with each step she took.

My eyes followed her as she made her way out the door.

Once Amarie was out of the room, I motioned for Wang to have a seat. I sat back in my chair and looked at him. He wore a black shirt and dress pants. His glasses were thick as fuck, and I swore his ass was getting on my nerves just sitting there at a loss for words.

"I know you may not want to work with me because I've been putting you off and standing you up when it comes to our business meetings—" he started.

"Which is bad for business." I cut him off.

"I know, and I'm sorry. If we're being honest here, I fucked up. Being afraid got in the way of my chances with you. I have had a lot of people turn down investing in me because of the fact that I'm gay, and I know how to talk numbers with people and get the amount I deserve. I'm good at what I do, and my family is depending on me. If I lose your offer, my family loses everything, and I am not trying to have that. I'm willing to work my ass off and make sure that the money you put into my family comes back to you, plus more. I'm not even looking for a handout. Shit, a loan will do me justice if you do not want to invest. I can pay you a percentage of every job I do as well as a check from the hair store each month. Whatever you want, we can do. Please, just give me a chance," he said.

If he never told me he was gay, I probably wouldn't have thought it. To me, he looked like he hacked computers and created bombs or some crazy shit. I knew he talked back to his parents. He had a lot of sass in him.

"I hear all that, and I know the kind of pressure on you, but that should make you say fuck the world and make you want it even more. Nobody can stop my grind, and ain't a muthafucka gon' out hustle me. I don't care if you like boys, girls, or whatever else. As long as you don't like kids, I'm cool. However, don't let what you like define you. I like green shit, and my favorite is the blue bills. Nobody is coming in the way of that. You have the hustle, but you don't have the mentality, and that's what I'm worried about. I get you're young and have some growing to do, but when you step to people, that age shit goes out the window," I schooled him.

I had been making money since I was younger, and I had the hustle and mentality of a young, broke nigga trying to make ends meet. I never let the money in my bank account make me comfortable. My goal was to retire by the age of forty, raise my kids, and work when I wanted to. At thirty-five, I wanted to be married and vacationing while running my businesses from home.

"You're right. I'll tell you this. The stuff I need will cost me about fifteen grand. If I can come to you with it in two weeks from working, can you help me? I have the mentality you're speaking on. I know I do, based on the simple fact of how bad I want it. I can see myself decorating celebrity birthday parties and even doing their make up if they need me to." He smiled.

"That's the mindset you got to have. Know you gon' get it regardless, with my help or no help. I'll tell you what. I'm going to give you ten racks in cash right now. You can use it how you see fit. However, in three weeks, you need to be able to come back and show me some kind of progress you made, and you know I ain't talking about no little shit either. I want you to take your first big check and put it where you think it belongs. Meaning, buy more into what you need, help your parents, whatever. If I like what you're doing, I'll begin the investment stage. If not, you pay me my money back when you can, and we move on in the business world without a partnership." I told him some real shit that had him unable to do anything but nod his head.

"Okay, do you need me to sign anything to say we agreed on this?" he asked, and I shook my head no.

"This place is covered in hidden cameras. I have enough footage," I admitted.

I saw the hunger in Wang, and that's why I didn't mind helping him. It was the same hunger I used to have. I knew even if I turned him down, he wasn't going to give up. It would be a better investment if I showed him how to make his money work for him. I pressed the code on the drawer next to me, and it opened. I handed Wang two neatly stacked piles of money— each had a piece of paper that read five thousand on it.

Wang's mouth dropped. "Dude, I've never even touched this much money before in real life, only on board games. I'll keep in touch with you. If I start to get on your nerves, please let me know. I want to thank you for this opportunity. Even though I can see this money may not mean nothing to you, it means a lot to me. I'm very appreciative of what you just did for me." Wang placed the money in his dumb ass briefcase, which I didn't even know people still used.

"Cool. Just do right by that shit. Don't make me regret it." I stood and shook his hand before walking him out of my office and to the elevators.

On my way back to my office, I stopped at Britt's desk. She was on her phone laughing, and she knew how I felt about that. Now, if she had her AirPods in, I would not have stopped, but she had the phone glued to her ear, loudly laughing like a ratchet ass young lady.

"Now, you know damn well that can get you written up," I said like I was not her boss.

"Girl, let me call you back." Britt quickly hung up her phone.

"My bad. My AirPods died," she apologized.

"Then you should have hung up. You loud as fuck, like this is not a place of business. I usually have to talk to the bitches at the front desk and the ones who clean up about shit like that, not you. That is not good for my business, and you know it. Let's not let that slip up happen again, or I'm sending you home."

Britt looked at me and nodded. I needed her to understand that she was working in the front of my office, and when people came and went, they saw her.

I walked to the back and went to the room where Amarie told me the clients I needed to meet with were. Fixing my suit jacket, I walked into the room.

"Hello, I'm sorry for keeping you waiting. I'm Kasha, and it's nice to meet you both." I extended my hand to the man first. After we shook hands, I shook hands with the lady before taking a seat.

"I see that you're interested in buying this house. How are we going about that?" I got right to business.

"Well, we have been approved for the first-time home-owners grant, and we've also managed to save fifteen thousand. I know you are asking for one hundred and fifty thousand, and that's fine, but how do we go about paying it off to you?" The guy spoke up for them both.

"That's cool. Usually, I do a straight buy. However, we can work out a deal. Before anything, I would need to run both of your credit. How do you both earn your income?" I spoke to them.

"I'm a registered nurse. I have paystubs and all. I also have a foster child, which I call my bonus baby. I receive a payment for her once a month," Alicia spoke.

The guy was now quiet, so either he didn't have a job, or he was in the streets. That was none of my business, as long as my money came on time.

We put a plan in motion, and I wrote everything down. Before they left, I had gotten Britt to type up the contract, and we all signed. They walked out happy, and I felt good, knowing I had just helped a family start the journey to owning their own home. I felt like I got a lot of work done, so I went back to my office and grabbed my things.

I knew Amarie was still working, so I left her alone. It was still early, so I went to Amarie's favorite restaurant, which was Chili's at the moment. I grabbed her the seafood Alfredo and a bowl of loaded mashed potatoes with no bacon. I drove home and placed her food on the counter. Going into the basement of the house, I went inside my mancave, which was my favorite part of the home. It was designed to my liking, and I found peace there outside of work.

After turning on one of my favorite movies, *Soul Men*, I grabbed my food, kicked my feet up, and ate. I sipped my Gatorade while stuffing my face. Placing the food on the table, I leaned my head back and enjoyed the peace and quiet. Sometimes I needed moments like this because it gave me time to reset. I was away from everything and enjoying time by myself. Something my father taught me at a young age was, you didn't need people to enjoy life. All you needed was yourself, and that's how I felt.

CHAPTER FOURTEEN
AMARIE

I closed the office door and locked it. I missed my man, and I was tired of beefing with him. Kash was in the bathroom, and his music was playing loud, so I was sure he hadn't heard me come in. I stripped out of my clothes, keeping my heels on, after removing everything from his desk. Then I climbed on top of the desk, spread my legs, and played in my neatly waxed pussy.

Kash walked out of the bathroom and looked at me with a smirk on his face.

"Oh, that's what you on, baby mom?" he asked as he looked down at me and smiled.

I kept my fingers moving in circles on my clit, making myself wetter. Picking me up, he pecked my lips a few times before sliding his tongue into my mouth. I returned his kiss with as much passion as he put into it.

"I'm sorry, baby. I don't want us to keep this shit up. I miss when we were happy with each other. Just tell me what I need to do, and I'll do it." I pulled away from him and looked him deep in the eyes.

His length grew against my legs as we kissed, and his hand found its way between my legs. He rubbed my clit in a circle, applying a little pressure.

"Take my last name then. Become my wife. Nobody has to know. Stop second guessing me. I'm your man, and you talk to me. You understand?" he asked.

"Yes," I moaned.

He placed his lips back on mine, and we shared yet another passionate kiss. I moaned into his mouth as he rubbed my purring kitty.

"You want me to give you some of this dick, don't you, baby? You miss me fucking you?" he asked.

I nodded. I missed shit like this, and I was dying to feel him inside me.

"Put that shit in, then." He grunted as he pulled his dick out of his slacks.

I gripped him in my hand and placed the head at my entrance. He pushed it in and took it out.

I was dripping wet and wanted nothing more than to be filled with dick. I didn't even care if the entire office heard me. They knew how I got pregnant. Kash lifted me in the air and set me on his shoulders. He was lips to lips with my second pair. I cried out as he tongue kissed my box. I would have preferred a quick dick down, but I loved the way he ate me too.

Kash swirled his tongue around and then up and down. Using two fingers, he spread my lips and slurped on my pearl.

"Oh, you doing your big one, daddy. Hmm, that's right. Eat that shit," I moaned while biting my lip.

My back was against the wall, and I was glad because my head fell back, and my legs began to shake. I rocked into Kash's face as he pressed his tongue harder and flicked it faster against my clit, making my body lock up like he always did.

"Arghhh, shit!" I screamed.

Kash looked up into my eyes, sliding one finger inside me then pumping it slowly. I held onto him for dear life. I felt like I would pass out and fall if his other hand left my waist. He kept his finger pumping at a fast pace as he used the tip of his tongue against my clit at the same pace as his finger.

"Shit!" I let out as I came in his mouth again, and he licked it all up.

Sliding me down his chest and onto his dick, he bounced me up and down.

"Oh, shit." Kash groaned in my ear. I slowly rotated my hips while he bounced me, causing him to tighten his hold. "I missed your ass too. I swear to God, I did," he growled in my ear. He held me against the wall, spreading my legs as he pounded into me.

"Ohhh, hmm, fuck!" I moaned loudly into his ear.

Kash loved the sound of me moaning. He always said it did something to him.

"I love you! I love you!" I cried as I bit his shoulder.

Kash let out a low moan as his body crashed against mine in slow, steady circles. He walked me over to the desk and laid me on top of it. I got on all fours and tooted my ass in the air, showing off the perfect arch.

He entered me from behind while pushing my back down. Kash grabbed a handful of my hair and used it to pull my head back and wrap his other hand around my throat. I threw my ass back against him while sucking on his finger that had touched my mouth. I was showing off with the way I tossed this big ass around, throwing it in circles, bouncing that thing up and down, and making my ass loudly clap against his stomach.

"Throw that shit back, bae, just like that. Hmm." Kash growled and slapped my ass.

He stuck the tip of his thumb in my butt and started

pounding into me. He knew that shit drove me crazy. I gave him all I had.

"Cum for me, daddy. You gon' cum for me?" I loudly moaned.

I was on the verge of cumming again, and this time, I wanted him to cum with me.

"Argh! Yeah, baby. I got you. Don't fucking stop! You better not fucking stop." Kash gripped my ass and slammed into me hard, damn near making me fall. However, I held onto the desk and threw my ass back, taking his dick like the pro I was.

Kash shot his load inside me as I came all over him. He then climbed off me and sat in his chair while I lay across the desk. At that moment, I knew there was nobody for me but him, and this was exactly where I wanted to be—butt ass naked in heels on my man's desk.

"Come on. We got work to do. Get up." Kash tapped my leg.

I slowly got up. After pulling my heels off, I went into his bathroom and cleaned myself up. I could hear someone knocking on the door but decided to finish what I was doing. Kash was out there, and he could open the door when he was ready.

I slipped my clothes back on, brushed my hair up into a messy bun, and walked out of the bathroom. Kasha was fully dressed, and his mother, Mrs. Kristie, was sitting in the seat across from him with a smile on her face. I was surprised to see her outside alone without Mr. Isiah.

"Nice to see you and my grandbaby. When are you coming to visit us?" she asked as I walked out of the bathroom and gave her a hug.

"Soon. We are trying to get everything situated here with my situation," I let her know.

Kash wanted to fly out and surprise them, but that had all

changed. I was on bail and I couldn't leave the state. Even if I could, I was too scared.

"Okay, well, when you get that figured out, we can talk about it. I wanted to also ask if it was okay if we threw you a baby shower. I was supposed to ask at your auntie's party, but girl, she had me lit. If it's okay, I'll ask her if we can do it together. This is my first and only grandchild, so I want to go all out. I hear Javon is the only one who knows the gender, and since I'm the glam mom, I feel like I should know too if that's okay with you. How have you been eating? Do you have any cravings? I have been eating pizza and hot Cheetos with ranch on it, which is crazy because I don't even do spicy," Mrs. Kristie went on.

I had to laugh because that was what I ate on my way into the office today.

"Yes, I eat that. I had it earlier. Kasha don't really like me having too much stuff like that, so I mainly eat healthy. I have been drinking a lot of water and keeping myself hydrated. Javon is the only person who knows, and if you want to know, then he can tell you. I just do not want to know yet. I want to focus on my child being healthy, not what she or he is. I am almost positive that I do not want to have a gender reveal party. Yet, a baby shower would be lovely. Kasha expressed that he did not see a big deal in having one because our child will have everything. So, as long as he's okay with it, I am too." I sat on the edge of the desk and sipped from Kash's water bottle.

"Kasha? Are you okay with a baby shower? I know I'm a little overly excited. I have been waiting for a grandchild for a while now. But I know how easy it can be to overstep when it comes to children, and I don't want to do that. So, if you guys aren't up to it, we don't have to do anything like that. I hear that you were a little further along than the doctors thought, which means we are halfway or almost halfway through this journey, but we still have some ways to go."

"Do whatever you want, Ma. I know if I told you no about a baby shower, you would be extremely upset. Make sure you include everybody in helping. How long are you and Dad down for?" Kash asked.

"We fly back in three days. Emily's ass is finally getting used to Florida, and I'm happy about that."

Hearing a knock on the door, I excused myself so I could open it. Britt stood on the other side with a big smile on her face.

"Hey, love, tell Kash Mrs. Miranda called. Oh, and let him know that Wang called for him as well. I know Mrs. Kristie is here, so I forwarded his calls for today. Oh, and 6327 needs an exterminator. They are complaining of noise in the ceiling at night." Britt peeked her head in the door.

"Well, if it isn't my missing assistant. I almost thought my girl stole your job," Kasha joked.

"She's good, but she could never. I'm the best at this job, which is why I'm the only one who's ever had it."

"Okay. Reach out to Harry and have him go over there and check that out. Forward my calls for the rest of the day. Once my mom leaves, I'm leaving the office," Kasha responded.

"Heard you." Britt waved bye and was gone.

Mrs. Kristie stood, dusted her dress off, and walked over to Kash. She pulled him into a hug before she walked over and did the same to me.

"I'll leave you all to your work. I will be contacting everyone for this baby shower. The moment we choose a theme, I will let you both know, so you have the final say. I love you both and take care." Mrs. Kristie rubbed my stomach before she left.

"You know Miranda was probably reaching out because of

your case. Do you want to call her, or do you want me to do it?" Kash asked.

"Go 'head and do it. Just put it on speaker, so I can hear." I walked back over to Kash's desk and climbed in his lap.

He dialed her number before placing the call on speaker and wrapping his arms around me. Miranda answered on the fourth ring.

"I was just pulling up to your office. We can do this over the phone, though, so I don't have to come all the way up. It seems that DeJuan and Nakari were having sex in the hotel room before he died. Her DNA was found all over his naked body. Because he had no smoke in his lungs, it was determined that he was dead before the fire. They had matching drugs in their systems. His phone also indicated that they were having a sexual relationship, so her accusations would've been unreliable at best. I could easily make this look like a jealous cousin, especially since there were a lot of messages of him speaking to people about messing up with Amarie. At this time, I have a few leads to go on. I'm going to go through each one, and whenever I get some information, I'll be sure to let you all know," she informed us, and I smiled.

"Thank you. I appreciate it," I told her.

Kash hung up the phone and kissed my lips.

"Everything gon' fall right into place," he told me, and I believed him.

CHAPTER FIFTEEN
VON

"Von, we cannot keep doing this. We are hurting each other. I do not want to end up destroying a friendship because we cannot be good to each other. We clearly aren't ready to be in a relationship," Natalia said, and I can't even lie; I was shocked.

This shit came from out of nowhere. I didn't respond to her. I just stared off into space. It was a lot to take in. I thought plenty of times that was what I wanted, but to hear her say it was a lot to handle. I was a player, so I couldn't even let it show how fucked up I really felt about it. I knew I had the potential to be a great man to Natalia, but my ass had so many fears that I would fuck it up that I kept fucking up. I swore on everything that Natalia and I would never come to this point because we were so much alike, and we didn't care about even really having a title on shit. I never even thought feelings would get involved because, at first, she was just another bitch, and I was the same for her—another nigga with money.

"You sure you ready to give up the realest nigga on your

team?" I made a joke out of it, when really, a nigga was hurting inside.

"Am I sure? Not really, but we have to. We only gon' end up hating each other, and I really do not want us to come to that. It's gon' be hard because your dick is amazing, and maybe one day you'll find a girl who will make you ready to settle down and start a family. That is where I'm trying to build myself to get. It's like we both want that, but maybe it's not the right time for us. That doesn't mean I ain't gon' miss that dick. I ain't gon' lie; that shit is dangerous, yet so good." She laughed through the tears that were falling down her face.

I was standing between her legs while she sat on her dresser. My hands rested on each side of her legs as I looked into her eyes. She was really serious, and I wasn't sure how I was going to take this. I had gotten used to coming home to her every night and sleeping next to her. I barely went home, and I was about to take my ass back. I would have to get used to not waking up to food in the morning and hearing her non singing ass be loud while getting ready for her day.

"You low key fucked me up with this. I was not expecting you to say no shit like this to me. I'm sorry for the shit I did to you. My intentions with you were always good, except when we first kicked it. I'm not gon' lie like I was not just trying to fuck, but your vibe made shit different. We clicked instantly, and that shit was wild to me. I don't be expressing my feelings and shit, and I know now shit is too late. Babe, I ain't even trying to change your mind on how you feel or what you standing on because you right. I ain't giving you what you need in a man, and I ain't trying to hold you back in life. I still want to be the nigga to bring you flowers when you graduate. That shit ain't changing. I want the best for you, love," I admitted.

"You making shit so hard. You was supposed to do that

nonchalant shit you be doing and just leave, so I can block you and ignore you. Not stand here and be so understanding," she said.

Natalia was still crying. However, she laughed and rolled her eyes at me.

"You better not ever try to replace me either. This shit we got is deeper than what I like to admit. I fucks with you. I just don't know how to be a man and show it. You gon' forever be in here. You own that shit for real," I said and tapped my chest.

"And that's stamped," she joked.

We shared a laugh, and then I leaned in and kissed her lips. She was going to at least let me get some pussy one last time before I packed my shit up and went on my way.

"We might as well fuck one last time, right?" She kissed me before leaning back against the dresser.

My dick always bricked up whenever Natalia kissed on me or touched me. I rubbed my dick a few times as I locked eyes with Natalia. My teeth sank into my bottom lip as I continued to rub myself. I had my dick in my hand, ready to give her the dick of her life. She was on some 'let us just be friends shit,' and I couldn't do anything at all but respect it.

I got on my knees after stripping out of my clothes. Now, I was between her legs, face to face with her pretty pussy. I didn't know how she thought we were going to make it through life without fucking from time to time. I bent her knees slightly. Lying on my stomach, I started to lick on her thighs. I wanted to tease her this time instead of diving right in. I kissed up her thighs, stopping each time I made it to her coochie.

"Stop playing and eat this pussy if that's what you gon' do." Natalia moaned.

I gave her what she wanted by spreading her pussy lips and licking her clit. Then I flicked my tongue on it before sucking it into my mouth. The way I moved my tongue so skillfully had her squirming and screaming that she was ready to cum. The moment she tried to scoot away from me, I dragged her ass back across the bed and began to suck on her pearl.

Grabbing her ass, I held her in place while licking and sucking on her. I smiled to myself when her back arched off the bed, and she got silent. Her body began to shake, and she came in my mouth. I lapped that shit up and then stood. Using the back of my hand, I wiped my mouth and began to grab my clothes so I could leave like she had requested a few minutes ago.

"Where the fuck you going? I need some dick. You know you can't just give me one without the other," Natalia whined.

Shaking my head, I laughed at her before giving her what she wanted.

"Grab your ankles, Nat, and you bet not let them bitches go either," I said with a low gaze. She did exactly what I said with her freaky ass. I knew she would be hard to get rid of. "Spread 'em, babe."

She looked at me with a weird expression but again did as I said. I sat on my knees with her head between them. My dick was touching her lips, so of course she licked it with her wild ass. What she did not expect was for me to wrap my arms around her and begin to eat her ass and pussy in that very position. If she wanted to leave me, I would let her. However, she would have a whole lot to remember.

It became a competition for us—who could out please the other. She was trying to suck the skin off my dick. Her mouth was so wet and warm. This girl could win a dick sucking competition. She was deep throating me while, humming at the same time. I felt like a bitch since my moans were damn near stuck in my throat. I was grunting and growling loud as hell. Maybe she was thinking like me. If this was our last fuck, we would give it our all.

Once I had enough, I got off Natalia. I laid her flat on her back and got on top of her. As I kissed her lips, I slid inside her. I grabbed one of her legs and wrapped it around my waist. She wrapped her arms around me as I dug deep into her.

"Ohh, baby," she hissed.

I went as deep as I could inside her, and somehow her legs ended up on my shoulders. We were tongue kissing now, and I swear it felt so right. Yet, we were no good for each other.

"I love you. Oh, God, I fucking love you!" Natalia screamed.

Her nails were digging into my back. I grabbed a handful of her hair as I pumped inside her with deep, long strokes. I licked and sucked on her neck while she clenched her walls, squeezing my dick. I knew her neck was gon' have all kinds of marks, just like my back. She was screaming with pleasure, and the shit sounded so good to me. We locked eyes, and I had to admit I felt exactly what she was screaming a few minutes ago.

"I love you too, Nat," I whispered as I came deep inside her.

I lay there for a second before I stood. Looking around the room, I let out a low sigh. Natalia lay on the bed, balled up. Leaving the room, I jogged down the stairs and grabbed a few trash bags before walking back up. I started going through the drawers and grabbing my things, tossing them into the trash bag. I didn't even realize how much shit I had until I was filling up my fourth trash bag. The last bag I did was my sneakers. I even went into the dirty clothes and got my shit from there.

Finally, I walked into the bathroom and took a quick shower before dressing in a pair of Nike sweats and a Polo t-shirt. I grabbed all my shit from the bathroom and tossed it in the duffel bag I brought with me the first time I stayed the night.

Then, I started taking all my bags downstairs, so I could take them to the car. By that point, Natalia was sitting in the middle of the bed, watching me. We did not say anything to each other the whole time. I guess everything we needed to say had already been said.

When I grabbed my last bag, I walked over to Natalia. Lifting her head by her chin, I kissed her lips.

"You bet not ever change for nobody. Your vibe is one of a kind. You're an amazing girl, and I'm just a fucked-up nigga. Hopefully, when I change and become a better man, it will not be too late. I love you." Dropping her key on the bed, I didn't even give her a chance to respond.

I walked out of her room and down the stairs.

For the first time in my life, I felt like a bitch had me ready to cry. Climbing in my car, I sat there and looked at her house. When I looked up, she was standing in the window, watching me. She wiped her face, and I knew she was crying. I started my car and put it in drive as a lone tear fell from my eye. Natalia was the only girl I ever said I love you to, and I blew it.

I knew this was something that would always have me mentally fucked up. When we first got together, everything was all laughs and games. We were always trying to outdo each other, but that shit quickly changed, and I always wanted to play the back while she shined. I now knew why Kash was the way he was over Amarie. I could see the stress in her eyes every time I fucked up and she made the choice to forgive me, and I didn't want to see that in her. I wanted her to be happy, and right now, it wasn't with me. That shit hurt real bad.

CHAPTER SIXTEEN

NATALIA

From where I stood, I watched Von pulled off. For a second, I thought he was going to walk back into the house, climb in the bed, and go to sleep while I got ready for class like he usually would. Instead, he pulled off. Instantly, I began to question myself on if I made the right decision. Von would always mention how much he cared for me, and he even showed it. However, when he looked me in my face and told me he loved me, my whole world shook.

Walking away from the window, I went into the bathroom and took a shower. I had three more months of school left, and I was going to give it my all. I didn't give a damn what I had to do. I was tired of depending on men and using my body.

Nakari's situation gave me the push I needed to do what I had to do. I was extremely hurt behind her death. I remembered talking to her before she went to jail.

It was a Saturday morning I would never forget. I was sitting in my living room, folding clothes. Nakari used her key to let herself in. When she saw me, she just broke down in tears.

"What's wrong, sis?" I asked.

"Life. It's fucking me up. I be so jealous in situations, and I don't want to be. Look at you. You're going to school and changing your life around. You have Von there supporting you. Then, look at Amarie. She is growing with her business and has Kasha, who's head over heels for her. My situation was over before it really started. I am fucked up behind Capri, and I don't even know what I want to do with my life. I hate feeling like I be feeling. It's always been like this too. I always felt like I wasn't enough, or I was competing with y'all." She admitted some shit I didn't know.

"Why would you be competing with us? We are your sisters and got your back. We do not have to compete with each other. We are all in our own lanes. Figure out what you want to do. What do you like to do?" I asked her, and she shrugged.

"I'm going to figure it out, and soon. I'm going to make you proud." She smiled, but her smile didn't reach her eyes. I knew she was crying for more reasons than one.

I wished I had picked her brain more and made her tell me what was going on with her. Now, my sister was dead, and nobody knew what was bothering her. She had turned to drugs, which wasn't so crazy to me. Nakari was always the one out of all of us who tried shit first or was down to do shit. Of course, we all smoked and drank, but Kari popped pills and did whatever else she wanted to do. She was just like my mom, and I believed that's why it was hitting her so hard. The child she turned up with and who was for all her dumb shit was gone.

Nakari was the only one out of all of us who wanted the fairytale, happily ever after kind of love. Amarie getting it was probably what caused her to try and ruin shit for that girl, which was completely wrong.

Turning my shower on, I let the water heat up before I stepped in. I cleansed my body and let the water wash away my tears. I cleaned my face, making sure to take my eyelashes off in the process. I was going to make a complete change. Grabbing my wig glue remover, I scrubbed the front of my wig, loosening the wig glue. Eventually, my wig was off. After taking my braids out, I washed my hair and conditioned it. Finally, I shut the water off, wrapped my towel around my body, and went to my bathroom counter.

I brushed my teeth and washed my face before I sat there for a while, blow drying my hair. Once it was completely dry, I got some Echo gel and ran my hands through my hair, so it would curl up. I brushed my hair into a bun, pulling my baby hairs out. Once I went into my bedroom, I put lotion on my body and slipped my clothes on. I grabbed my Ugg shoes that looked like Crocs and placed my feet in them. Then, I went back in the bathroom and slicked my edges. Looking at my reflection, I smiled at myself. I looked like the younger me.

Grabbing my book bag and my car keys, I went outside to my car. I had about thirty minutes to make it to school. I got to class early and sat in front instead of in the back like I usually did.

When the teacher walked in, she smiled at me.

"Okay, nice to see you in on time and ready to learn. I don't know who this new person is, but I hope she is here to stay," she joked, but I knew she was serious.

Just last week, I was getting in trouble for coming to class late and missing some of my work. I had also failed my last test, which was the only test I had ever failed. I didn't like the feeling, so I was making sure it didn't happen again. Minutes later, everyone started piling into class.

"You in my seat," Angel said when she walked in.

"I never knew we had assigned seats. I made it here first, and this is where I want to sit. So, this is where I'm going to sit," I calmly replied.

I wasn't trying to go there with her because this was only day one of my change, and I was not trying to go back this soon. Plus, fighting in school would jeopardize all my long, hard months of work.

"Everybody been sitting in the same seats. You need to get up before I move you," she spat.

Looking her in the face, I laughed. I was not about to argue with her, nor was I getting up to move. If she attempted to move me, I was for sure going to beat her ass.

"What's the problem, Angel?" Ms. Yates questioned.

"This bitch is in my seat and won't move!" she barked.

She was feeling herself, and I was not sure why. Ignoring her little comment, I continued to sit there while she ranted and stomped her feet like a kid. I didn't care what she said, as long as she didn't touch me.

Angel grabbed my book bag and tossed it across the room. I quickly stood up from the chair and pointed my finger in her face.

"I'm going to ask you nicely to go get my shit. Now I sat there and let you run your movie. You done called me all kinds of bitches and all. I ain't say shit. What you not gon' do is disrespect me. Now, if I throw you like you threw my bag, I would be wrong." I tapped her forehead with each word.

"Angel, that was not okay. Get that girl's damn book bag and leave for the day. You are disrupting my class." Ms. Yates raised her voice.

Angel picked my bag up, and I snatched it from her. The good lord knew I wanted to beat her ass. Everything in me told me to knock the bitch out, but that's what she expected. She wanted me to throw away my schooling because that's exactly what would've happened had I fought her. Sitting back down, I got my books out and got ready to learn. Class took longer than usual because we were starting to learn hands on things and not just book work, letting me know that the finish line was close.

Once class was over, I got in my car and drove to my mom's house just to check on her. When I pulled up, she had the door wide open with the fly net thingy hanging so no bugs could get in. I stepped inside and found her sitting on the couch smoking. The smell of food had me going straight into the kitchen. After washing my hands, I made myself a plate of food before sitting at the table to eat the mashed potatoes and steak that my mom made. I noticed that she had blown up a big picture of Nakari and placed it on the wall. A pink and purple urn was on the shelf with some flowers and candles around it.

"You okay, baby?" my mom asked as she walked in, puffing on her cigarette.

"Yeah. I almost got into some shit at school. This bitch threw my book bag 'cause I sat in her seat when we don't even have assigned seats. I wanted to beat her ass, but I am on some new shit. How you holding up?"

"I'm literally just taking it one day at a time. That's all I can do. I miss her, and I love her. This, we all know. Yet, it was her time, and I can't keep questioning God about that." My mom took a pull of her Newport.

I knew she smoked weed, but cigarettes were crazy. I kept fanning myself, and she eventually put it out.

"I love you, Mom, and you did a great job with us. Please stop blaming yourself," I told her, and she broke down in tears.

I needed her to stop. She did right by us; we did wrong on our own, just like most people. We were kids, young adults, still learning. Nakari's addiction just seemed to beat her in the game of life.

CHAPTER SEVENTEEN

KASH

It was early in the morning, a little after seven, and I was still in bed. Amarie had made me breakfast, which I had finished very quickly. I was surprised she was even up this early because that girl always slept in late. I didn't know if Amarie knew I meant what I said about making her my wife, but I was ready to show her.

Climbing out of bed, I slid on a pair of jeans since I had already taken a shower. I pulled a black Polo t-shirt over my head and headed down the stairs. Amarie was already dressed in a pair of yoga shorts and a graphic t-shirt that had Boyz in the Hood on it.

"Put ya shoes on. We have to run somewhere right fast," I said and handed her the slides she had been wearing lately.

I stepped into my black and white panda dunks and waited for her. Amarie finished cleaning up the kitchen, and we walked out the door, hand in hand.

We got into the car, and I started it. Amarie reclined the seat and closed her eyes. When she yawned, I knew her ass was tired and would be due for a nap soon. I drove straight to the courthouse, and by the time we reached it, she was out cold.

"Baby, get your ass up." I tapped Amarie on her thigh, and she stirred a little but didn't wake all the way up.

"I'm tired. Go in the store without me. Nobody can see inside your car," she said, keeping her eyes closed.

"Get your ass up. Let's go," I said a bit more sternly.

Amarie sucked her teeth but got up and out of the car. I walked around and grabbed her hand before walking her into the courthouse.

"What the hell we doing here?" she asked me with a look of concern.

"I was serious about you being my wife. You thought I was playing?" I asked.

"Baby, we could have at least gotten dressed." She playfully hit me.

Grabbing her hands, I pulled her to me and kissed her lips.

"We good just like this. I only brought you and me because nobody has to know we married until we have a big wedding if that's what you want," I told her.

"I'm cool with just this," she replied, and we walked to the desk.

We told the guy what we were there for, and he told us where we needed to go. An hour later, we were called to the back.

"Do you have a witness?" the guy asked us, and we shook our heads no.

"You all need a witness," he said.

I walked into the hallway and saw an older lady walking by.

"Excuse me, ma'am," I said before approaching her.

She stopped and looked over at me.

"My name is Kasha, and my girlfriend, who is pregnant

with my child, and I need a witness to get married. We are trying to do things the right way and be married before the baby comes. Unfortunately, we didn't know we needed a witness. If you have extra time on your hands, would you mind helping us?" I asked.

"Oh, sure, honey, and congrats," she said and followed me.

"Here's our witness." I walked over to Amarie and held onto her hands.

"Okay, so we are ready then. I'm going to get straight to it. What are your names?" he asked.

"Amarie and Kasha," I answered.

"Do you, Kasha, take this woman to be your lawfully wedded wife? To live together in matrimony, to love her, comfort her honor, and keep her in sickness and in health, in sorrow and in joy. To have and to hold, from this day forward, as long as you both shall live?" he asked.

"Yeah," I replied, and Amarie burst out laughing.

"Baby, you supposed to say I do," she whispered.

"Oh, my bad. I do." I fixed my answer.

He repeated the same thing to Amarie, and she quickly said, "I do."

"Before these witnesses, you have pledged to be joined in marriage. You have now sealed this pledge with your wedding rings. By the authority vested in me by the great State of Pennsylvania, I now pronounce you married!" he shouted with excitement.

The little old lady loudly clapped while I kissed my wife. I was happy that now when I called her that shit, I wasn't just saying it. I walked back over to the lady and thanked her.

The man let us know that the paperwork we had filled out in the beginning would be sent to us in the mail. Amarie was finally carrying my last name, and that was the best feeling a nigga had since hearing she was having my baby.

We walked out of the building a married couple. I couldn't believe we really did that shit. I always talked about it, but I didn't know she would be as serious as I was. While we were there, I asked Amarie multiple times if she wanted me to buy her a ring once we left, and she said no. She was fine with just having my last name until we had a wedding in front of everyone. I loved that about her. She was so simple.

We walked back to my car, and this time, she got into the driver's seat.

"Where you trying to go?" I asked.

"I don't know. I just wanted to see if you was going to let me drive. I honestly don't even feel like driving." She laughed and climbed out of the passenger seat.

I walked around the car while her ass climbed over my seats, knowing I hated that shit. I got in the driver's seat and just sat there staring at her. This girl was really my wife.

"Can I get some dick right quick?" she asked.

"In front the courthouse?" I smirked.

"Yeah, you have mirror tint. We good."

"Look at me." I pulled her into my lap. Once she had her shorts off, Amarie looked me in my eyes. "I love you," I told her as I slid her panties to the side.

I pulled my dick out of my boxers and stroked it a few times before I slid inside her.

"I love you too," she gasped.

I lifted my hips, digging deep inside her. She was screaming how she felt him in her stomach. Amarie began to move her hips in a circular slow motion, riding my dick like she should have been doing. Her feet were on my shoulders, and her hands were on my knees. Her hips rocked back and forth, leaving me access to rub on her pearl. I used my thumb to play with her clit while I sucked on her neatly painted, pretty feet. This was my wife, so I was going to do all the nasty shit to her.

"Ohhh, fuck, baby!" she cried.

Amarie leaned forward and wrapped her arms around my neck. She placed her feet at my side as she bounced her ass up and down on me.

"That's right, baby!" I held onto her hips.

She licked my bottom lip, and I stuck my tongue out, allowing her to suck it into her mouth. We kissed as she slowed her pace while riding me. I reached on the side and leaned my seat back, so she would have more space. Amarie placed one leg on my shoulder and the other leg stayed down, so it looked like she was in a split. She rocked her hips while I held onto her leg with one hand and her ass with the other. Her head was on the middle console, and I used that as my opportunity to fuck the shit out of her.

"Arghhh! You going too deep!" she screamed and tried to get up, but I held her ass still. She should have never gotten in that position.

I kept thrusting forward, harder each time. I was grunting, and she was moaning.

"Shit, this shit is too good," I mumbled as I pumped inside her.

"Throw that shit, baby." I slapped her hard on her ass.

Lifting Amarie up, I flipped us over, so she could be the one lying in the chair. I climbed back between her legs and slid inside her. Since my nut was already right there, I fucked her until I came.

"That was supposed to be a quick ride," Amarie said as she climbed into the other seat and fixed her clothes.

I didn't know when or how it happened, but her panties were ripped in half.

"My bad," was all I had to say.

Once I put my dick back in my pants, I pulled off. I was now hungry and wanted something quick, so I drove straight down

Walnut Street to Wendy's. There were a lot of places I could have stopped. However, it would have been a hassle finding parking and a meter that worked.

"You already know I want some spicy and regular nuggets." Amarie smiled.

She had this thing where she dipped her nuggets in her Frosty, and the shit was actually good. I ordered our food and paid. The line was short, and the food was hot. We drove back home, and when we arrived, her mom was sitting on the steps.

"I'm gon' beat this bitch's ass, bro. I swear." Amarie huffed.

Reaching in the glove compartment, I handed Amarie an envelope with her name on it. She looked at it before opening it. The brown envelope had stacks of hundred-dollar bills in it. It was the money I was going to give her to merge our companies plus some. She looked at me then back at the money.

"Pay her ass, so she can leave you alone," I told her.

Amarie grabbed a stack of hundreds and began to count them. I quietly watched her as she counted ten thousand dollars. We stepped out of the car together after she put the rest in her bag.

"You know why I'm here," her mom started.

"If I give you ten bands right now, can we call it even? We do not ever have to speak again. If not, I'll pay you in installments of twenty dollars a year. As long as I am making payments on the amount that we agreed on, you can make no moves," Amarie said.

Her mom's eyes lit up at the mention of ten thousand dollars. In my mind, her ass had to be getting high or something because she was money hungry. She had her mom verbally agree on video that she would take the ten thousand in cash and leave her alone. Amarie handed me her phone, and I watched her count the money. Each time she got to a thousand, she handed it to her mom until she had the full ten thousand in her hand.

"Now, get the fuck from in front of my door. Please do not ever speak to me or come around me again. You did not even have the decency to ask me if I was all right or if your grandchild was okay, not once. You ain't nothing but a money hungry old lady. I want to be so disrespectful to you, but my heart won't allow it. You mean me no good, and I do not want to deal with your kind." Amarie was on the verge of tears.

Her mom looked at her with sad eyes before she turned and walked away without saying anything. I knew Amarie's words hurt her, but not enough for her to say sorry or be a mother. Her mom hopped in the driver's side of a car and pulled off.

"Why is Miranda here?" Amarie asked as our lawyer pulled in and stepped out of her car.

"I'm here because you, sir, have to go pick up a check for her bail money, and you, ma'am, are cleared of all charges. DeJuan's mother brought a recording down to the district with Nakari's confession. We are going to make sure your record is clean. I hope that makes your day. I see baby must have you emotional." She motioned to Amarie's face, which was full of tears.

"All the time. Thank you. I'll be sure to pick that check up. Shit, that's twenty-five bands that I can do something with."

"Thank you, Miranda. I appreciate you and your hard work. You're great at what you do!" Amarie cried as she ate her chicken nuggets.

Miranda smiled and went on her way.

I walked into the house with my wife, happy that two weights were now lifted off her shoulders, and she could spend the rest of her pregnancy focused on the baby and building our businesses, and nothing else.

CHAPTER EIGHTEEN
AMARIE

I woke up bright and early to a message from Kash, telling me to meet him at the airport. I didn't understand why I was doing that, but instead of complaining, I washed my ass, threw on something comfortable, and drove to the airport. Once I got there, I called his phone twice, and he ignored me both times. Instead of answering, he told me to come to the Delta terminal and leave my key with Big Red. I drove around until I spotted Big Red. Climbing out of the car, I have him a small hug before handing him my keys.

"I'm going to have this parked in front your house," he said, and I nodded.

I walked inside the airport and smiled when I saw my aunt, Natalia, Von, and my dad with luggage.

"Where Kash at?" I asked them as I gave everyone hugs.

"He's here somewhere. I know we have to get going." My aunt pulled me toward the security check in.

She was in there acting like she'd never gone anywhere before, so when she wasn't looking, I rolled my eyes at her. I knew not to do that shit to her face because I was sure she would still try to hit me. Ann didn't care how old we were; in her mind, we were never too old to get a beatdown.

I didn't have anything but my pocketbook, and I was glad I brought that along with me. Natalia handed me a boarding pass just as Kash wrapped his arms around me from behind. I did not have to turn around to know it was him. I knew his scent and just the safe feeling I got in his arms.

"I figured we all needed a getaway. So, I'm flying y'all out. We will be gone for about six days. We are first going to Miami to meet up with my mom and dad. Then, we will fly private to Bali. I want this vacation to be peaceful and fun for all of you. We will be staying at a resort, so don't let Bali owe you nothing." Kash gave a whole speech to us, and everyone was excited.

My man was doing his big one, and I was going to make sure I let him have me how ever he wanted, when and wherever he wanted. I was going to get flewed out and slutted out. We made our way through all the checks and screenings before we were seated on a two hour trip to Miami. I could not help but notice that Natalia didn't have on an ounce of makeup, nor did she have a weave, which was shocking. Natalia had that pretty, curly hair that had me always thinking she was mixed with something. She was in a natural state, and she looked so beautiful. I also peeped that she and Von were not up under each other like they normally would be. I laid my head on Kash's shoulder and drifted off to sleep. I didn't really like long rides, so I always slept through them.

"Baby, wake up." Kash tapped me.

Rubbing my eyes, I opened them and looked around to see everyone starting to stand with their luggage. Kash, Von, and I were the only ones without clothes, and I wasn't feeling that. However, I did know that meant I would get the chance to go shopping in Miami, and I was going to get real cute. I planned to have Natalia style me because a bitch was due for a new look, and that girl could dress her ass off.

Being back in Miami reminded me of how Kash and I met. That man was and still is so fine to me. Even when he was sleeping with his mouth wide open and drooling, that man was gorgeous. And he was all mine. We headed off the plane and went to baggage claim. Kash talked on the phone with his mom for a while. I could hear him telling her that we were at baggage claim and about to come out as soon as everyone got their bags.

"Ann, what the hell you got in this suitcase?" my dad asked my aunt.

He yanked her suitcase off the baggage carousel and dropped it on the floor. I didn't even know why he was doing that when he knew he wasn't in any shape to be lifting heavy luggage.

"My shit. Kasha, Kristie out there? I need to smoke," my aunt shouted like that was okay.

Kash laughed but told her yes. Once everyone had their bags, we walked outside. I loved how the air was different. The sun was shining, and there was no breeze. Pulling off Kash's hoodie, I handed it to him.

"It's hot as hell," Natalia said.

I spotted Emily's ass as she ran toward me. She pulled me into a hug before rubbing my belly.

"I can't believe I'm going to be an auntie. I'm gon' spoil this child so much. Oh, I have my license." Emily flashed her driver's license.

"Okay, boo! How you been doing down here? I see you finally enjoying it," I questioned her.

"Yes, I am. And the boys here have way more money. I mean, they make Philly niggas look broke."

"Not my man, but yeah, most Philly niggas are broke. They

just pretend they not. Don't be focused on these boys, though," I replied.

We climbed in his mom and Emily's cars and drove back to her house. Kash, Emily, Von, Natalia, and I all stayed in the car because we needed to go to the mall. While we were there, I would use the time to ask Natalia what the hell was going on.

Natalia looked at me, and I motioned for her to look at her phone. I had texted her, asking what was going on, and she only sent me the eyeroll emoji back. I needed the tea, and I wanted it hot and steamy. Outside of Kash and me, they were my favorite couple. That was mainly because when it was time to do something, I knew who Von was gon' bring as a date, and I didn't have to get to know the person.

Once I realized she wasn't going to tell me, I left it alone. I was determined to get the truth out of her, but for now, I was about to shop until I dropped. We arrived at the mall, and I immediately went to Saks. Messing with Kash, this store was slowly becoming one of my favorites. The first thing I did was pick up a pair of YSL heels. They were the Cassandra sandals in patent leather with a gold-tone monogram. I had seen them online, but when I went to the store in Philly, they didn't have them. After getting the salesperson to put the shoes behind the counter for me, I walked around to see what else I wanted.

"You have to get these Miami platform Gucci shoes, bitch, since Miami is the place that turned your life around." Natalia pointed to the shoes, and I got them just because.

"Baby, you like these?" Kash was holding a pair of mint green Amiri slides in the air.

"Yes, that color is cute." I looked at a few bags and grabbed something to match the shoes I picked up.

I also grabbed some perfume. When I got to the register, Kash was there waiting for me. He pulled me to him and smiled.

"You got everything you wanted?" he asked as he handed the lady his card.

"Yeah, for the most part. I didn't really see too much in here."

We continued to shop around until my feet were hurting.

"We board the plane at six. I want to get to our destination on time, so be up and ready." We headed into the house, and I climbed into the bed in one of the guest rooms.

As soon as my head hit the pillow, I fell asleep.

CHAPTER NINETEEN
NATALIA

"Y'all bitches looking real good and natural. Amarie, that glow on you is something else, though," Emily said as we lay in the sand.

Bali was so pretty. The water was clear, and each room had its own private pool outside. Well, at least the ones we had.

"Girl, this place is beautiful, and you look good too. You think you grown. Kash gon' curse you out with that little swimsuit you got on," Amarie pointed out as she sipped her virgin drink.

"I ain't worried about him." Emily laughed as she fixed her shorts and began to do a few Tik Tok videos.

"What's up with you and Javon?" Amarie asked me.

"Girl, nothing. We just better off as friends. We not trying to hurt each other, which we were doing. That's still my guy," I admitted.

Von had the key to my heart, and it was no taking that back. However, I couldn't keep holding onto something that wasn't right for me. No matter how much I wanted it to be, it wasn't.

Today was the first day in Bali, and I did not want to spend it talking about Javon. It was bad enough that our rooms were next to each other. Just like now, we were all in the pool, and he came out looking heaven sent. Today, he had on a pair of Gucci shorts, and his bare chest was on full display. I kept imagining my hands rubbing up and down his chest while he fucked me on one of those beaches. Everything there was beautiful, and I could tell Kash spent a lot of money to take us there. He even put us in our own rooms. The island we were on was one to remember, and I never wanted to go home.

"We supposed to have a private dinner tonight as well as get massages or some shit. Y'all know I can't do too much, so the girls will be getting rubbed down while the guys go ride ATVs. I think that's where they are all headed now. Mrs. Kristie and Auntie Ann went with them. You know they wasn't gon' miss nothing like that. I'm sorry y'all had to be stuck with the pregnant chick." Amarie pouted.

"I'm cool with that, as long as we can go to the other pool, and I can get my drink on. I'm going to need a drink with the way Javon been acting," I admitted. Hell, I cared more than I would have liked.

"I'm married," Amarie let out, making me choke on my drink.

"We know that. I mean, you're technically a widow, right?" Emily questioned.

"My husband is very much alive. Kash and I got married. Please don't tell nobody. I wasn't even supposed to say shit until we were ready to have a big wedding. However, we done already went down to the courthouse and got married." Amarie smiled.

My cousin looked so happy talking about it, and I loved that for her. She deserved every bit of happiness she was getting.

"Bitch, you done got married and pregnant in less than a year. I see you acting out." I gave her a high five.

We sat around gossiping until it was time to head back to our rooms for our private massages. By the time I got up, I was already drunk. As I approached my room, I saw a lady standing in the hall with a bunch of bags.

"Natalia? I'm Rose, and I'll be doing your massage," the lady introduced herself.

We walked into my room, and while she set up, I took my swimsuit cover-up off. Lying across the portable massage table, I closed my eyes while the slow music played from her speakers.

"You like rainfall?" she asked, and I nodded.

The sound of rain always relaxed me. Seconds later, the sound of rain was playing, and it was that hard rain.

"Relax," she told me as she started to rub my back and shoulders.

Her hands felt so good that my mouth slightly opened. She rubbed my whole body down, and the shit felt amazing. I didn't know how much American money was worth to her, but I was definitely giving her a hundred-dollar tip. The way her hands skillfully moved across my body was crazy. She was using her elbows and all, paying attention to the spots that hurt me as well as what she called my stiff spots. Being the girl that I was, I lifted my drink and sipped from the straw.

When she finished, I got up and gave her a nice tip. She packed her stuff up and I went to take a shower. I could hear Javon laughing as I stepped into the shower. I knew they were back, and I would have to find a quick time to talk to him without everyone knowing what was going on. I quickly washed up and slid on another bikini to make it look like I was about to go for a swim. Going to my pool, I sat on the side, allowing my body to soak up the sun. Javon could be heard laughing at someone. I smiled when I heard him say that he was enjoying himself.

Javon was leaned against his railing, smoking a blunt. Not having anything to say to him, I thought of the dumbest shit to do. I dropped my lighter over the railing.

"You have a light?" I asked, but he ignored me and continued to talk on the phone.

"Javon!" I called out to him. He looked over at me and waited for me to say something.

"My lighter fell. Do you have one I can use?" Javon laughed but handed me his lighter. I used it to light my weed before handing it back to him.

"Yeah, that's my people. No, she needed a light. How you figure I'm playing games? I'm just not on that right now," he said.

Yes, my ass was listening to his conversation.

Javon looked back over at me since I had told him thank you. He gave me a head nod and kept talking. Not liking that shit, I put my weed out and walked back into my room, so I could go to his. Javon was so nonchalant that it didn't make any sense. I grabbed the bottle of Hennessy and turned it up to my lips. I was going to knock on his door and let him know he was fucked up for treating me like I didn't exist. That wasn't how friends moved.

Once I started to feel hot, I walked out of my room and knocked on his door. I waited for a second before I knocked again, this time a little harder.

Javon opened the door with a mug on his face. His hand was clutching his gun, and I was trying to figure out how he even got it there. Then I remembered we stopped in Miami and flew private.

"You gon' let me in?" I asked.

Javon stepped back and let me inside while he continued talking on the phone.

Grabbing his weed out of his hand, I walked outside and lit it. I sat on the side of the pool, smoking while splashing my feet in the water. A few minutes later, he came and sat next to me. He was no longer on the phone. I handed him the weed and just stared at him.

"Fuck you want from me?" he questioned, blowing a cloud of smoke in the air.

"I don't know. Why can't we still be normal and talk to each other? Exchange hug when we see each other. You've been giving me the silent treatment since before we got here. I still text you every day, yet you don't respond. I'm not trying to be your girl or get on your nerves. We can be friends," I said.

He shook his head with a laugh.

"Nah, we can't be friends. You wanted shit like this, and I respected your hand. You didn't give a fuck, really, about how I felt. My ass was fucked behind you. How I'm supposed to carry on with you like nothing happened, Nat?" he replied.

"It's like you want to come here, get drunk, and have me still be all over you. In Philly, you did everything in your power to duck me. I'm not gon' chase you, baby. I'm not that nigga. I fucks with you too much, and that's why we can't be friends. When I'm around you, I want do shit to you that friends don't do to each other, and I have to distance myself from you for a while until I'm over this shit," he kept going.

I nodded then leaned over and kissed his lips.

Javon didn't stop me. Instead, he deepened the kiss. It had been a while since I had tasted my dick, and my mouth was watering for it. I probably would always end up fucking Von, and for the moment, I was okay with it. There was no way we would avoid the inevitable on this trip. As much as I told myself to stay away from him was as much as I watched him. Javon was completely ignoring me, and I hated it, which was how I ended up knocking on his door, ready to confront him. I hated that he was making things so obvious. Granted, we weren't a couple, but we could still be friends and have fun together.

"Come here, Javon. You said that was my dick forever, right? Well, I want to suck my dick, please," I pleaded, looking up at him through my thick eyelashes.

Javon looked at me and shook his head before walking outside to his private pool. Stomping behind him, I wanted to curse him out. He smirked then pulled his dick out, motioning for me to suck it.

I dropped to my knees and grabbed his tool in my hands. Licking him from the base to the tip, I made sure my mouth was really wet while I jerked him off. Javon was leaning back against the sliding doors. For a while, I focused only on the tip, swirling my tongue around it and applying as much pressure as I could. After spitting on his dick, I made sure to smack it on my lips.

I licked all the way down, using the topside of my tongue. I couldn't forget about his balls, which seemed to be his most sensitive spot. While his dick was down my throat, I stuck my tongue out and licked his balls. That motion made me gag, so I pulled back, allowing all the spit to fall on his dick. I sucked his balls into my mouth for a second and then licked them. All the while, I kept stroking his dick with both hands.

I could have been a paid porn star with the way I was showing off.

"Argh, fuck." He moaned and grabbed a fistful of my hair.

Von began to fuck my face, and I let him. I pecked my way back up to the mushroom shaped head and slightly opened my lips, so I could gently suck the head between them. I licked my lips, getting them really moist with my spit, then I ran them over his dick up and down before slurping him into my mouth.

"'Mmmm," I moaned as I reached down and began to rub my dripping wet pussy.

"Oh, my fucking God. Damn, Nat!" He groaned and began to pump into my mouth as I deep throated him. I refused to not give him the best head in the world.

He shot his seed down my throat, and I swallowed most of it. The rest, I used to make spit bubbles and blow them back on his dick. I sucked on him until he was back hard.

Javon pulled me up to my feet and walked us over to the little bar that he had set up near his pool, which my room didn't have. He stood between my legs, pushed my bathing suit bottom to the side, and entered me. I wrapped my legs around his waist, moaning at his forceful entrance.

"Give him to me, daddy. Fuck me like you miss me too." I moaned, licking his ear in the process.

Javon grunted and continued to stroke me. I leaned back on the bar, and he pulled me to the edge, lifting my legs straight in the air. Javon licked my leg while he slammed inside me.

"Javon!" I screamed. He was filling me up in every way. It felt like his dick was touching spots in my stomach that I never knew existed.

"Stop bitching. You wanted this. You came knocking on my door after you said fuck me. I'm about to cum." He growled and smacked my hands off his hips. His thrusts were powerful and fast.

We came together, and then he let me down, smacking my ass in the process.

"Those legs looking a little shaky, my man," I told him as he leaned against the bar, staring at me.

I could see a mixture of hurt and anger in his eyes. I quickly grabbed the shirt he had on earlier and tossed it on. Then, I left his room, afraid he would tell me to get out.

Once his door closed behind me, I realized I had fucked up and did not grab my room key when I left. I stood in the hall for a while, not knowing what to do. I didn't want to go back to Von's room, yet I wasn't trying to be caught in the hall, wearing nothing but his shirt. Knocking on everyone's door produced nothing. I stood out there for what felt like ten more minutes before I went back to Von's door. I knocked, and he opened it right away.

"I forgot my key in my room. Can I just chill in here for a little bit?" I asked.

"Yeah," he replied.

Javon walked into the bathroom, and I heard the shower come on. I didn't feel like standing by the door, so I went into the bathroom and grabbed one of the rags from the pack he had. I wet the rag in the sink and wiped my feet off. Then I hung it on the rack and climbed into Von's bed. I must have drifted off to sleep because I did not remember Von coming out of the bathroom.

"Aye, you can lay on the couch, friend. A nigga trying to go to sleep," he stated, being smart.

"Your dick was just down my throat. Wasn't shit friendly about that," I countered.

He had a towel wrapped around his waist with beads of water falling from his chest. If my pussy wasn't still sore, I would have jumped on his ass. I kept telling myself that we needed to be friends, but my actions weren't matching what I was saying, and neither were my feelings. I had talked a good game like I always did, but he was showing me why he was always in charge.

Javon climbed in bed next to me once he saw that I was not getting up. Just like he always did, he pulled me to him and connected our legs. Von slid his arms around my waist, holding me extremely close to him. I felt so content in his arms, and it scared me. I knew that shit with us could end up one or two ways, and while one was good, the other was bad. I felt like I was having an internal battle. My mind said he was no good for me, while my heart was beating fast, and my body relaxed against him.

"I love you, friend," Javon said before I heard his light snores.

I closed my eyes and tried to go to sleep with him.

God, if he ain't no good for me, why you keep letting me go back? I know it's my fault because I won't leave him alone, but it's hard. I feel like I belong here with him, and I know he feels it too. I can tell by how he looks at me and how he holds me, like now. Please, God, if he's the one for me, don't let me ruin it. Oh, and thank you for everything. I know my sister is in a better place, and I know she's happy and content with Capri. Please protect the rest of my family that's on this earth and allow them some sort of happiness. We deserve it. Javon does too, and please keep him safe and protected while he's in those streets.

I said a silent prayer, hoping it was something like Ciara's prayer when she got Russell. 'Cause, if not, I was signing myself up for a crazy heartbreak.

CHAPTER TWENTY
KASH

The entire time we were on the trip, I had been secretly planning a surprise wedding. While everyone thought we were doing a late night dinner, they wouldn't know what was really going on until it was happening. Britt had flown out to help me get shit together. So far, she was doing great with staying under the radar. Like, now, I was lying in bed with Amarie, while Britt was out with Emily, picking up last minutes things.

"Did you ever think we'd be here, baby?" Amarie asked as she rubbed her belly.

Lying in bed, doing nothing, we were able to just vibe with no TV or anything, just enjoying each other's presence. Looking at Amarie, I just shook my head. I honestly only had intentions of helping her and being her friend. I never meant for us to end up in love, but I didn't regret it.

"Nah, we've been through some shit, and if we being honest, this is only the beginning. I'm willing to go through every obstacle with you if you willing to go through it with me. Shit, once feelings got involved, I started hoping that one day we'd make it here. You were who I was meant to be with from the very start," I confessed, nuzzling my face into my baby's neck and making her giggle.

"I feel like that when it comes to you too. I know some people feel like we're moving fast, and I question it too at times. Then again, we're moving at our own pace, and nobody has to deal with this life but us," Amarie said.

"I have to go make sure the front desk has the damn reservations and shit ready. I just forgot I had to go down there and pay them people," I said, climbing out of bed.

I found anything to say to wrap up our conversation. I needed to get away from her before I slipped up and told her what I was really up to. Grabbing a pair of Nike shorts and a Nike t-shirt, I slid my clothes on and headed out to Natalia's room. That girl was a beast at makeup, and I needed to ensure she did Amarie's. Even though it was going to be a small wedding, pictures would be taken, and I wanted my wife to look good.

"Sis, you up?" I lightly tapped on the door.

"Yeah, bro, what's up?" she questioned.

I laughed. She and Von swore they were done with each other, but his ass was trying to hide behind the door like a kid.

"I need you to do everybody's makeup for me tonight. Do not forget it's a nude color theme. Emily is out at the strips if you need anything. I got a check for you too," I told her, and then I addressed my silly ass homeboy. "I should push the door and hit your big ass with it. We all know y'all can't leave each other alone. Ain't nobody judging y'all." I laughed at them as I walked out.

I made my way to the front desk of the resort to make sure the section of the beach that I had rented was ready. They told me they had decorators and all. This was another thing I had Britt and Emily doing—making sure their event planners were on point. Of course, they wanted to have bottles and all kinds of other shit, which they had to go and get. I wanted an open bar, so it was easier for me to just buy a bunch of Hennessy and shit that we drank.

"Hello, I wanted to speak with Carlos about the section of the beach I rented. My name is Kasha." I spoke to the receptionist.

"One second," she told me.

I stood there and waited until a man dressed in pink shorts and a white and pink flamingo shirt came out.

"Hello, I'm Carlos. Come on, let me show you what I have done so far." He led me out the side doors.

We walked a short distance, and I had to smile. There were chairs lined up neatly on both sides of a little walkway. In one chair was a picture of Nakari tied to the seat. I didn't know whose idea that was, but I didn't say anything. I just hoped it didn't fuck up Amarie's mood. They had a little arch set up with red, white, and some other color roses going around the top.

"I am going to put some lights here next to each row of seats, and red rose petals down the aisle. Over there is where the tables will be set up, so everyone will see that first and still think it's a dinner. Britt wants you and a Mr. Aaron to arrive last. He's going to ask to talk to her while Emily brings everyone over to the seats. Of course, music will be playing," he said, and it all sounded good to me.

"Oh, and the colors on the table will match the nude themed dinner," he added.

We walked back inside, and I swiped my card, paying the remaining balance for everything. I tried to pay it all upfront, but they wouldn't let me, which was dumb to me. I made sure to leave a nice tip because ole Carlos was doing his thing. When I got back to the room, it was three in the afternoon.

Amarie was out with the girls, doing some shopping for their outfits while I gathered the guys to do our shopping.

"Mr. Aaron, I need a huge favor from you."

I pulled Amarie's dad aside as we headed out to the cars. He and my dad had clicked on this trip, and all they did was smoke cigars and gamble.

"What is it?" he asked.

"First, I need you to grant me permission to marry your daughter," I said, like I really needed it.

I had already married her, but today was her big day, and I wanted to ask him.

"Of course, you can. Shit, I feel like you would have done it either way." He laughed.

"I would have. Another thing, I am going to marry her tonight, and I need you to keep it a secret. I need you to act like you want to talk to her, then, when you get the signal, which will be a slow song, bring her out," I said, and he nodded. I just hoped he didn't fuck it up.

We all got our clothes and headed back to the resort to get dressed. The dinner was at eight, and the time seemed to be flying by. I did not have any time to go back and check on things, so I could only hope that everything was done the right way.

———

"Yo, you ready?" Von asked.

"Ima meet you down there, bro. My shit bubbling. I ain't trying to be at no dinner table like this," I said as I sat on the toilet.

I didn't really have to go to the bathroom, but I had to give him some reason for staying behind.

"Damn, bro, make sure you wet the tissue before you wipe

your ass. I don't need you having on no nude with a splash of chocolate," Von joked.

I waited until I heard him leave the room before I came out of the bathroom.

I had on a pair of nude-colored slim-fit slacks with a matching blazer. I left the blazer open, showing off my white shirt, which was left unbuttoned at the top. My shirt was tucked in my pants, and my white Ferragamo belt with the silver buckle was on full display. I had on a pair of white Ferragamo shoes, and a pair of Cartier glasses sat on my face. While we were in Miami shopping, I purchased Amarie an eighteen-karat white gold hidden halo diamond ring. It cost me about fifteen thousand dollars. I had it in my pocket, playing with it.

My phone rang, letting me know to come downstairs. As I made my way, I did my best to avoid everyone seeing me. I watched from the side as Mr. Aaron talked to Amarie. Due to the way he had her standing, I was able to ease out the side door while everyone else was seated by Emily.

"I'm so proud of you, son!" my mom cried as my dad took a seat next to her.

I placed my finger to my lips, not wanting her to be too loud.

It's undeniable
That we should be together
It's unbelievable how I used to say that I'd fall never
The basis is need to know, if you don't know just how I feel
Then let me show you now that I'm for real
If all things in time, time will reveal
Yes

When the music started playing, everyone looked back, and Mr. Aaron was walking Amarie out the door. She had on a white dress that looked to have a little lace at the top, and her pregnant belly was on full display.

"Oh, God." She stopped and began to cry.

Mr. Aaron pulled her arm and led her down the aisle. The sun was setting, and the whole scene was beautiful. I quickly wiped my face before a tear could fall. I met Mr. Aaron, and he handed his daughter off to me.

"You could have told me," she whispered.

"You look beautiful," I responded.

We stepped in front of the preacher, and he did a whole bunch of talking, to which I was not listening. I regretted not eating anything because my stomach was growling, and I wished he'd hurry up.

"Kasha, I understand you have some words for your wife."

I cleared my throat and let out a breath. *Here goes nothing.*

"You continuously think I need you to do more for me than you already do or that I feel like you are not thankful. At times, I did feel that way, but that was before I considered you thanking me by holding me down. You never question me when I am out handling business and tor I'm out doing something with another bitch. You don't be stressing me. You've kept me happy with the amazing sex and homecooked meals. By making sure the house is clean when I get home and having the clothes washed, all the while carrying my child. You're giving me the baby I've always wanted. Hopefully, it's a girl, and that's enough right there. I love you for that.

"I grew to love your drive and how dedicated you were to becoming something. I fell in love with your light snores at night and the way you look in your bonnet while in bed. Baby, if there was any girl in the world standing next to you, I'd still choose you. Now, stop crying 'fore you mess up your makeup," I said as I used my thumb to wipe away her tears.

She grabbed my face and kissed me passionately. I could

tell she wanted to put all her feelings into that kiss. I responded by just simply holding her face in my hands and putting my own emotions into the kiss. Pulling away, I had to catch my breath. I smirked at her and laid my hand on her belly. The way she made me feel was amazing, like she was one of the many pieces that I needed to be genuinely happy. The money, cars, and everything I had meant nothing to me when it came to her.

I pulled Amarie's ring from my pocket and slid it on her finger. It fit like a glove.

"God damn, baby. This bitch shining," she said like the preacher man was not a few feet away.

"She sorry," I said and let him finish his speech.

Once he was done, we all went over to the table and began to eat. I took shots with the guys and even got cursed out by Natalia for not letting her help with the planning. I knew her ass would have spilled the tea or whatever that shit was they said. For the remainder of the night, we had fun and partied. The night couldn't have gone any better for me.

CHAPTER TWENTY-ONE

AMARIE

K ash had me on cloud nine. I was completely surprised and blown away by his actions. We were now back in Philly, and all the fun was over. It was time to get back to work. I sat at my desk, remembering how he had me bent in all different ways in that Bali sand.

Kash climbed between my legs and eased his dick inside me. I moaned at his entrance. His dick was extremely big, and as much as we fucked, I could never get used to it.

"That dick feels good, don't it, wife?" he asked as he placed one of my legs on his shoulder.

Once he found a steady pace, he kept it. I was grabbing at the sand, and all it did was fall through my fingers. I bit my lip, trying to hold in my moans as he hit every spot he was supposed to. I did not want to be too loud since we were dipped off on the beach, and everyone was still partying.

"Let that shit out, ma," he told me while rotating his hips.

"Fuck, I feel it in my stomach!" I screamed, hoping the music would mask our lovemaking sounds.

"That's where you supposed to feel him," he told me.

Kash flipped me over and started hitting me from the back. I threw my ass back at him, trying to make him cum fast so we didn't get caught.

"Let me hear that shit," Kash told me, smacking my ass.

I moaned loudly for him. The way he was stroking me, I had to scream and say fuck getting caught. The dick was just that good. Hell, I was pregnant; they knew what we were doing. I was throwing my ass back at my husband.

Kasha dug his nails into my ass cheeks. He even licked my back, which was exposed by the deep dip in the back of my dress.

"Lay back. Let me ride that dick." I moaned.

If I had to have sand all over me, so would he. He lay back and let me do my thing. I rotated my hips in a slow, circular motion while rubbing his balls.

"Baby, you gon' make a nigga bust," he let me know.

I watched as his toes curled, then I lifted myself a little and made my ass jiggle as I moved up and down on him like a stripper. I made my ass cheeks jump one at a time.

Kasha grabbed my hips and slammed up into me while I kept the same steady pace. Minutes later, we screamed in unison as we came. I stood up on shaky legs and dusted the sand out of my hair and off my clothes. Kash got up and did the same before he helped me get the sand out of my hair.

"Ain't you supposed to be home making dinner? Why you still here?" Kash asked as he walked into the office.

"Yeah, but we were supposed to leave together tonight. Remember, we came in your car? Plus, you didn't even take the steak out like I asked you, so you're going to have to eat something quick, or we'll have to stop by a fast food place," I reminded him.

Kash was starting to want me home more because my blood pressure was always on the rise. He also constantly wanted me to cook him something. I was trying to get him to at least start taking stuff out because, half the time, I didn't even know what he felt like eating. When he did tell me, it was always some shit I would have to stop by the market to get when he could have simply just taken it out himself.

"Amarie, these people at the front desk asking to speak with you. Something about a DeJuan," Britt's voice came over the phone.

I looked at Kash, confused as to why someone would want to speak to me about him.

"Let them in," I replied.

I took a seat on top of Kash's desk and waited to see who walked in. When DeJuan's parents walked in, I remained calm.

"Hey, umm. I just came to tell you sorry for how we treated you. I know it probably means nothing, but as DeJuan's wife, you are entitled to get all his life insurance policies and his trust fund," his mother spoke.

"Umm, I am Kasha's wife. As far as his life insurance policies go, you can keep them. I do not want anything from that man. I have everything I want and need," I let them know.

DeJuan's mother looked at my belly in disgust, and I only smirked at her. I meant what I said. They could have everything. I did not want anything from that man. I didn't want my name attached to his name or anything else for that matter. Whatever he left behind, he left behind. If it were up to me, they would never be able to access it. I wanted to be the bigger person, but at the end of the day, fuck them people.

"Okay. We need you to sign some papers releasing any claim to an inheritance," his mother replied.

"I am not dumb. I won't be signing anything until my lawyer looks over it. You can leave the papers or have them faxed over to my office. Here is my card. I wish you all luck, but please do not come here again. If the paperwork is legit, I will sign it and have it mailed to you. But please leave me alone and let me live my life. You guys caused enough trouble along with your son. I did not deserve any of it, and now you want to be sorry because you want that money. Truthfully, you can shove them sorries up your sorry ass," I lectured them.

Fuck them people and everybody with them. Had that man not died, they would still be trying to cause havoc in my life instead of teaching their son how to be a man.

They turned on their heels and made their way out of the office.

"Aye, Britt, don't ever let them back up in here," I called out, and she laughed.

"Bitch, get that money and give it to me. That is for pain and suffering," she called back.

"What I tell y'all about that?" Kash scolded us. He was always speaking on how we had to use better language in the office, but nobody was there, and nobody was coming. It was just us.

"We know. The language that we use outside the office is what we use outside the office. Inside the office, we need to leave the ratchet bullcrap at home. Inside Kasha's place of business, we conduct positive energy, and we speak great things into existence," Britt mocked Kasha, causing me to double over in laughter.

"I'ma see how funny it is when I fire both y'all asses. Just because you my wife and she is my assistant/little sis don't mean y'all can do what y'all want," he fussed.

"We know because if you let us do it, everyone will try to do it, and you can't have that inside this place where you have all sorts of clientele and business partners coming in and out. We know, daddy, but you still have to loosen up some. We are here to work. However, we deserve some sort of fun too. Your ass think you running a plantation or something," I told him.

I was forever telling Kash to loosen up a bit. Everyone

deserved to have fun once in a while, whether in their work-place or at home. Some people go to work to escape life, and he knew that because there was once a time when he said he came there to escape me. Work did not have to feel like work all the time. As long as you got your job done and got it done right, I was cool. And maybe that was why Kash's shit was running so smoothly. He had rules, and he didn't let anyone break them.

"I hear you, and what is this I hear about you giving the company a gathering? We need to talk about that as well," he said to me.

I quickly jumped up off the desk and grabbed my things.

"Take ya time in here, babe. Britt said she will drop me off at home," I lied through my teeth, and he knew I was lying.

"Stop lying. She ain't say that shit."

"Language. There is no cursing in this building. Not that loud, anyway," the janitor said as he walked by.

Britt and I thought that was so funny. Judging by his facial expression, Kash had just seen how strict he really was on how his employees behaved. He did not mind a little cursing here or there; it was the constant shit for him. When everyone started to do it, no matter who was around or what kind of meeting we were holding. His favorite line was he needed his crew to be able to turn it on and off at all times. Britt's ass even got away with playing music with a bunch of killing and cussing in it throughout the day. Hell, I sang along with most of the songs when I heard them, and he did too. He often played those same songs in his car or at home.

Kash was a whole different person when it came to busi-ness, though, especially his businesses. He did not play about his money, and I loved that about him. People from all over the place respected him. I also loved that he was not afraid to express his feelings about certain things. One of the things he did that I admired was helping Wang. Wang had been back so many times, telling Kash about his and his family's accomplishments and dropping off money.

Kash didn't even know I was thinking about expanding my business ventures and adding different things under our umbrella. I did not want to just stay on properties. I wanted to have my hand in a little of everything, but I was going to figure out what I wanted to do first, make a business plan, and show my husband to see if he agreed with me. He was my partner, and before I made any big business moves, I should speak with him first. He was still more groomed than I was, but I had proven time and time again that everything I got, I earned and deserved.

I made a one year stand a lifetime deal, and it worked out in my favor, even with all the bullshit that came with it. And I did it all the right way, securing a bag that was rightfully mine. I learned not to tell everybody every move, and it was certain shit that I would take to the grave. I was up and did not plan to come back down.

EPILOGUE
THREE YEARS LATER...

"Kashmere, sit your butt down!" I yelled at my daughter, who was in her terrible twos.

I wanted to chase her, but my belly would not allow me. Yeah, Kash had me knocked up again, and this time, I was carrying triplets. How we got there, I did not know, but I knew it had to happen when we went to visit his family in Miami.

While I wanted to be in the office, all that came to a halt when I could not find it in me to allow Kashmere to go to daycare. I had seen so many Instagram posts about things happening to kids that I was scared to let her out of my sight.

"Kash," Kasha called her when he walked in the door, and she ran over to him.

Watching Kash scoop her up into his arms, I hoped one of the ones I carried would look like me. Kashmere was the spitting image of her daddy, except she had thick, bushy hair that I found myself having a hard time combing. Which was why she was currently rocking a bush and a headband.

"Daddy, stop!" Kashmere yelled through laughter as he tickled her.

I was glad he had come home because it was no way I would be able to get her in the tub and wash her hair by myself. When her daddy was not there, that girl gave me hell, but when he came in, she acted like the sweetest girl ever. Kashmere had everyone in the family wrapped around her finger, which I knew would not be good once I had the other babies.

My businesses were going so well. Yes, that's right, *businesses*. Once we had my office running, we used that strictly for the rental properties, while Kash's place was for the homebuyers. Since cooking was something I could do at home with Kashmere, I began to make videos of me cooking and what I fed her throughout the day. Somehow, I had grown a following, and I eventually started getting checks from Instagram.

I had opened a little water ice shop that would be open all year around. I had all types of desserts and ice cream there too. I had found a girl who was baking in her home and did really well with cakes and pastries off Instagram named Miley. I hired her, and she had been doing her thing for the last three months.

A lot of people told Kash and me that we were moving too fast, but they didn't know us. They didn't see the love we had for each other. We had our days when we fussed and fought. However, that never stopped Kash or me from coming home at night. I did not have to worry about other females because Kash had proven his loyalty time and time again. Most people believed that all men cheat, and that's why I was so grateful my man was my man because he was all about me. Just like I was all about him.

"Bitch, why y'all have the door unlocked? Y'all know there are crazy people out there?" Natalia asked as she walked in.

"Because I live in a gated community where there is no trouble, and I can. I always wanted to be able to leave my door unlocked and not worry about some crazy shit happening," I replied.

"I don't give a damn where I live. I'm locking the door. You are crazy. Where is Kashmere? I know if she ain't running wild, that means Kash is here. His friend is not with him, is he?" she asked.

"No, Javon is not here. Why you keep playing with that man anyway? You be ducking him for two days, and then go jump on his dick. That's dumb as hell to me because y'all do this shit every two days," I told her honestly.

"I mean, ducking him was easy until this morning. I just got in good with my job. Hell, I just got a raise, and now, here I am, pregnant. I mean, abortion or adoption is always an option," she said like she was about that life.

"Yeah, so is death when Javon finds out and kills your ass. Bitch, you want to visit the upper room, you gone 'head. You should have been careful," I told her. She knew I was serious about Javon trying to kill her if he found out.

I didn't even understand why those were options when they both were extremely good with kids.

"Bitch, I can give them kids back. I cannot do that with my own. I'm afraid of failing, and I've never seen myself even being a mother. I'll probably be like Ann but without all the love." She wiped her tears.

"That's a mother's thing. I am afraid too, and I already got a baby. Now look at me, the size of a whale, going from one to four under four. You have to believe in yourself," I advised.

Natalia had graduated and had gone through her little phase. She did the big chop when we came back from Bali and had been rocking her hair cut low ever since. She and Javon had finally called it quits after one of his female friends dropped a baby off on him. I couldn't believe he was a single dad. Natalia was hurt, but she did not let that stop her from doing what she needed to do. I felt like she could have forgiven him because the girl was something he did when they were not together. However, in her mind, they were never apart.

That little boy was exactly what Javon needed because the moment he got him was the moment he decided to leave the game alone. I was super proud of him. He and Natalia were still messing around, yet she could not let that hurt go. Natalia did everything with Jasai. It was almost as if he was her son, which let me know that she was not really that mad at Javon.

We were all living our best lives. Was it perfect? No, but it could not have been better. And if I could do it all again, I would do another one-year stand with my billionaire. Not only did he take me from a broken-hearted weak girl and make me a strong, independent woman, but he also made me a mother, a millionaire, and the wife of a billionaire, all off a one-year promise.

THE END.

ALSO BY YONA

Made in the USA
Middletown, DE
05 July 2023

34598487R00092